Richard Aiyes is a British African, married to his beautiful wife, with four children: two boys and two girls. He has a wonderful daughter-in-law, and as of current, two amazing grandsons. He attended the University of East London, where he obtained a BA Honours Degree in Accounting and Finance in the year 2012. At the moment, he works as a security officer. He hopes to share a little bit of history with you.

This book is dedicated to my father, Chief Oluwo:
J E Aiyedogbon.

Richard Aiyes

MY WIFE AND
MINE ROD

AUSTIN MACAULEY PUBLISHERS™

LONDON • CAMBRIDGE • NEW YORK • SHARJAH

A CIP catalogue record for this title is available from the British
Library.

ISBN 9781786125576 (Paperback)
ISBN 9781786125583 (Hardback)
ISBN 9781528951807 (ePub e-book)

www.austinmacauley.com

First Published 2021
Austin Macauley Publishers Ltd®
1 Canada Square
Canary Wharf
London
E14 5AA

Prologue

A husband and wife are meant to be. They both go through ups and downs. They rear their children together to create their own version of history. This history passes on to younger generations.

This is how the Almighty wanted us to make history. Brothers and sisters make your own history; let your children have something to talk about when you are dead.

Remember your partner's love. Come down to their level.

Words of wisdom are better than rubies, silver and gold. Mind you, every man is the architect of his or her own future.

Introduction

My father was a very tall man – a man of stature – not fat and not skinny. He was born in a town called Bono and died in 1976. He had seven wives, four concubines and nineteen children. I can remember that he loved children so much that he wished he could have half a stadium full of people as his own children. When I heard that, I was amazed. I smiled and laughed. I knew it was his dream.

Usually, he always wore his white robe, made of about ten yards of 100% cotton, bought for him by one of my uncles from London. Whenever he got up from bed, he would walk about 500 yards before he reached the place where he used to sit himself every morning. Whenever he came out, before he reached his seat, the cotton robe – which spread for about 6ft around him – would be sweeping the floor as he moved forward. Thank goodness he always routinely made his wives clean the premises.

At his seat, the children would be called sometimes, in batches of about six or just two or three to greet him. The girls would be on their knees and the boys would lie down with their chests and chins touching the ground while he blessed them by praying to God for their protection, guidance and happiness. He would always mention in his blessings that we live a life without having to beg for food, and then he would ask us to rise up. He issued these blessings for up to 20 minutes – sometimes as long as 30 minutes! In fact, for us children, our morning blessings were more than enough to carry us throughout the week until we could top up at church on Sunday with more blessings from the priest. Personally, I believed that the blessings from the old man were enough and we had no need for going to church.

After I received my blessing on this day, I did not leave my father, he said to me, "Have a seat with me please. There are a few things you're going to do for me." He broke his speech to speak with his wife inside his bedroom, "Do you mind bringing with you my tobacco pipe when coming out?" He then turned to me, saying, "You, young man, kindly sit on the bench that is next to the chair. I always prefer my darlings seated very close to me. Not for any particular reason, but that is how I feel comfortable." He said it with amusement.

I smiled and he winked with his left eye – making him look very handsome. I wanted him to wink one more time, but those old people have a funny sort of way, so I said nothing and kept my thoughts to myself. Shortly after that, a lady of about 5ft 5ins came from the room. She was light brown in complexion with dishevelled hair. Of course, I vividly remembered that she was his seventh wife. We never saw much of the wives because we children stayed in a different location from the wives. So, we only saw some of the wives or our own mum occasionally, when they called for us or sent us out on an errand. Some of us didn't like him having many wives; we thought he should stop marrying after our mums but that was a definite and decisive NO.

Number seven wore traditional casual clothing. She wore a top and bottom, the blouse and the lapel (this wrapped around the legs), with a sandal shoe. Her nose was not flat like the typical African person. She must have been one of those who had blood connections with the Spanish or the British. However, she might have been the prettiest woman I'd ever seen, but her hair needed some styling by the city hairdresser. She eyed me, then without saying hello to her husband, just sat down on the chair in front of him.

"Where is my pipe?" he asked.

"Here," she passed it to him.

"What kept you so long?"

"You," she responded. It seemed the old man was trying to force a smile out of her. The situation was cordial amongst them because they both knew what they were dragging on about.

I thought to myself, *Perhaps it is time for me to leave and join my brother and sisters to play.* I stood up.

"Sit down there," he said in a loud voice, "I do not want you to go because I have got a lot to discuss with you. Make yourself feel comfortable. Has everybody had their breakfast yet?"

"No," I said.

"Looking at the time, it's going around 11 a.m. Mmmm, I have stopped my children from eating very early in the morning not because I am wicked. It's like when a father smacks a child, this is done in love. The time is coming when you children will be pleased with such an attitude because in the time of war, you'll be used to hunger and survival. Perhaps that attitude made me survive the war."

"Which war?"

"World War One and World War Two."

Gently, he looked away from me back to the pretty lady who had been quiet for a while, and they both winked at each other. Her blouse was open, and he thrust his hand into her chest coat and brought out her left breast. With a quick glance, I saw her nipple, which was about one-inch long. I took my eyes off her briefly and he said abruptly, "Why are you looking away? I like her breast so much that it drives me to bed all the time. Look, I am going to suck it. It's a pity you have not got a girlfriend, but even if you did, her nipples could not be like her nipples." The lady smiled and gave him a kiss and gently put her breast back inside the chest coat.

"I'm going to take a bath now. You need to bring your book and pen out. In fact, I have already got a writing pad here for you to use as you are going to write something down for me. See you soon," said the old man. He then went away with his wife to the bathroom that was built like a shed. Where I sat, I could see the side of the bath-shed. Then I stood and tried to have a good look while creeping forward a little. I could see the wife by the entrance of the shed, but his big robe was used as a door so that I could hardly see him inside. I went back and sat down.

Suddenly, his wife rushed out, and she asked me, "Are you alright?"

"Very fine, thank you," I replied whilst she dashed inside the house. She must have gone to retrieve something for her husband, who was still in the bathroom. I sighed to myself, relieved. She rushed back out again. The way she ran, I am sure that if anyone had been in her way, she would have run the person down. This time, I did not bother to consider what was going on. After ten minutes or so, they were out again. They both looked fresh and clean as if they had bathed together! *Eh!* I thought, *This old man is too much for me. He behaves like a person who has been abroad for years in the UK or America.*

"Alright, young man?" he asked me.

"Yes, Pa, you look fresh and clean."

"Many thanks, young man, I am very verily cleaned," he responded with a great smile on his face, that showed that he could joke around. To make quick comments in front of elders is not our custom, even a compliment was not permitted, but he was an Old Boy not a grumpy elder. "I will not take much of your time; I am very sorry for the delay."

"Never mind," I said and with that they both disappeared into the bedroom. If I hadn't known him, I would have said he was taking the piss. I had still not yet eaten. But, looking back, his behaviour was nothing short of an exciting interlude, which now makes me laugh at moments when I remember.

Eventually, he came out on his own and was very well-dressed. "If time doesn't take a job," he said, "a job should not take time. There are some stories I would like to tell you. You may like to write them down but it's actually up to you. In this case, I will ask you, have you eaten?"

"Yes Pa, I've had my breakfast. I didn't require anything except to drink water from the tap."

"Hooooo," he laughed. "You are not expensive to treat. If I come to you, you need to dig into your pocket. If I don't make a hole in your pocket, you'd be lucky. Okay, shall we get to business?"

***

Chapter One

Chief Hunter, Little Hunter and Tes

"This season is one of the best I have ever seen since I was born. Every time I get out there, I always kill and kill animals," said Little Hunter.

"Yes! Yes! Yes, my Little Hunter, exactly!" said the Chief Hunter.

"Boss, let me go home and clean this animal that I've killed and cook it."

"Also, for your information, Little Hunter, none of today's killings are going to the palace."

"That is all right by me, Chief."

"Not every day, every day is not Christmas, and not all the time do you have to give food to King," continued Chief Hunter.

"Chief, are you jealous of the King?"

"Of course, yes. Believe me, last Monday (Ojo Aje) you took to the King the leg of an ostrich. He told me about it. He said that you are a good boy and that since the death of your father, you are always bringing him legs – sometimes two legs – of animals, and he appreciates it very much."

"But, you are the head of the hunters. I also thank you very much for being loyal to me. God of Hunter, bless you, may the bush be easy for you." Saying that, Little Hunter turned his back and started on his way home. But he abruptly turned back and said to the Chief, "Why should I go home? I might as well stay here, go to the backyard of your house and clean the animals I brought from the bush – the two antelopes, pig and rabbit."

The Chief shouted back, "Call me when you finish the cleaning, then we can share it accordingly." After he had finished, Little Hunter let the Chief share the killings. Two legs of the antelope went to Chief Hunter, then two legs of the rabbit and the front leg of the antelope was put aside for the Deputy Chief Hunter. The rest was left for Little Hunter. "The leftover is too much. Let us share it equally," said Little Hunter, "Because I cannot get it cooked in time without it going rotten. I'm the only one. I am on my own so this all would be too much for me. Do you remember? Who is going to cook and eat with me? Nobody. I am alone and that is why I'm murmuring all the time when we are together. I need a lovely woman to cook for me." He chuckled when saying his last words. His chuckle sounded almost insincere, but not spiteful; he just seemed almost hurt that he didn't have a woman.

Then he cried, "Every day, I pray to have a wife – a woman who will love me and take care of me like my mother and father did, Chief." He stared directly in to Chief's eyes as though he was searching for clarification for his unanswered prayers.

"Let's pray, Little Hunter," said the Chief calmly. "The sort of wife that you are looking for, the God Almighty will provide for you." The Little Hunter cried Amen more than three times, then he got up and started on his way home. He left the rest of the meat for the Chief Hunter, who had a wife, Tes, but no children. Chief and Tes had been married for over two years. Chief shouted to Little Hunter, "See you, my little but big hunter! But, when next will I see you, because I will surely ask Tes, my wife here, to cook so that we can both have dinner together?"

Little Hunter replied, "See you in the evening then."

Little Hunter was a very short man of about 4ft 3ins tall. He looked as if he didn't know where a bathroom was to wash his mouth. His teeth were decayed and grey, with visible black tars that showed some greenish colour. In fact, it was disgusting to look at his face. Chief Hunter was more friendly looking but brutal in attitude. He didn't tend to look back on what he had hurt, nor did he take pity on anything.

After Little Hunter had left, the local youths were asking, "Chief, why does your friend look ugly and rugged?"

Chief said, "Little Hunter became like that due to what the bush has made of him. In the bush, you are alone and within a few seconds you are dead or alive. Moreover, when you are faced with a wild animal that needs its meal, that is terribly hungry, and is looking at you as supper or dinner, the fight is not easy. You cannot run or shout. Of course, noise cannot help, it even brings on more pressure that the other hungry predators will come. Children, you know, in the bush, we don't speak, but only occasionally we sing. We sing especially when we kill a big animal that we can cook for a big dinner or make money from." The Chief rarely directly answered questions and always thought it appropriate to lecture.

He continued, "When you are faced with a wild animal, the question is do or die. First, you must communicate with

15

your god and the other animal gods for survival, and that is the reason for our music – it could be loud or silent. Then we often get into the habit of eating raw leaves and other medicines for survival that may require you to wash them. If you don't find a stream or river and have already run out of water, the sort of medicines we use will damage your teeth for life within three to four hours of use. So, that is what you have seen on the Little Hunter.

"But does it not affect me like that, you're wondering? It depends on how individuals look after their body. As for me, I swim and bathe twice a day, especially when I go to bush. I often go to the stream to wash my mouth and my body; sometimes, we often spend a day or two or three, even a week in the bush before we come back home. Before I come back, I always make sure I swim and clean myself in a stream or river. I took to the habit of using a stem of a branch at the stream or river to brush my mouth and to chew on. I can never pass a stream or river without using the water to rinse my feet, mouth, face, armpits and underpants. But some hunters don't do these things."

The youth then asked, "Chief, where do you sleep when you are in the bush for weeks or months?"

The Chief Hunter replied, "I make a few huts out there on the trees and the ground. It depends. Sometimes dangerous animals sleep in the trees, right? Yes. There are tigers, leopards, cheetahs, pumas and jaguars. You have to be clever and use your medicine so that they don't see you." After explaining survival tricks to the youths, he continued with the conversation about Little Hunter.

Little Hunter returned the same evening to the Chief's house. When the Chief opened the door, he said, "Chief, I tried to freshen up myself for the dinner this evening, so that I can enjoy your wife's food." Could he have guessed or suspected that his friend had been discussing his demeanour with the young people? It was as if he had telepathically taken on the advice the Chief had given to the youth earlier on in the day.

Graciously, Chief smiled and replied, "I believe that is good. You are my little but big hunter – the famous and durable man. You should have your seat very close to me." They both sat together and ate quietly. Then they ate the bones of the meat, cracking them like dogs.

"You must finish everything," said Tes.

"No, I have had enough for tonight. Chief and My Lady, the food was delicious, many thanks," replied Little Hunter. Then Chief and Little washed their hands and moved away from the dining room. The Chief grabbed a keg of palm wine (oguro), and they both lit up their tobacco. The smoke coming through their nostrils was bluish. They both felt excited, enjoying each other's company.

Generally, when they conversed, they never spoke about when they would be hunting, because their skills were much more outstanding than the poachers.

"When next is our anniversary?" asked the Little Hunter.

"Well, still far away, roughly in ten to eleven months' times or so I think," Chief replied. They spoke of the Hunting Festival. It was said to be the most wonderful thing in the village and the town, for those who were lucky to witness it. There was always talk about it – about watching it again and again. This created great expectation for those who were yet to see it – children, adults, schoolchildren, visitors and strangers. Everyone was always talking about the Hunting Festival.

"I have got plan for the next anniversary party," Little Hunter continued, "It is going to be a special, remarkable occasion."

"Usually it is. If I remember correctly, you performed some of those magic that you got from your father at the last one."

"Yes indeed," said Little.

"And where did you get those people that held you?" asked Chief.

"They came from my father's hometown, that is Ilodi, and they were some of the best dancers in the world. In our land today, we have the best dancers," replied Little.

"So far, I do not have any plan. All I know is that we will do it as we did it last year and the year before. It is always the same, nothing so spectacular in it," said Chief.

"Hey, don't say that! Since I was a child, I have been enjoying the Hunting Festival, and when I grew up, I joined them and am part of the group. That was my father's wish when he was alive, and it has always been my wish to become a well-known and successful Little Hunter."

Seeing the distaste for the topic in the eyes of the Chief, Little Hunter changed the conversation. "My friend the Chief Hunter, you are quite successful; quite recently you received a call from the King that you would be crowned as the Head of the Soldiers of our town. Even if you were not paid, at least you would receive gifts that would be twice or more than my annual salary," said Little. Chief Hunter laughed in response, but his laugh was clearly forced and false. Sensing this, Little

Hunter walked away from his sight gently and quietly. "In fact, I reckon it's time to go home," said Little Hunter.

He popped inside to see Chief's wife and thanked her for the dinner and the evening. Whilst he was walking away, he continued speaking, "By the grace of God, this time next year we will celebrate the occasion with a child at your back. It's time for me to go home."

Tes said, "Please mind how you go, my Little Hunter. It's evening and evening does not know the noble man."

Little replied with "thank you" and waved goodbye.

***

Chapter Two

Little Hunter

Evening does not make any one of us hunters afraid. It's our daylight. Neither would Tes' husband be afraid because we're both the same. But, perhaps, I should have waited or slept tonight with Chief Hunter. Ah, home is home; it's time I should go home.

I was awoken by the sound of drumming and the sunlight that rose early in the morning. Not the cockerel crow. It didn't wake me. I was surprised; I must have had a sound sleep. But, where is the drumming come from? I sighed to myself. It must be from the King's palace; yes, of course. But that is about a mile and half from my house. On special days and on occasions when the King is usually visited, he is woken up by drumming. This is at least four to five times in a week. These are normally traditional occasions which may require his attention. We drum for our King as it makes him feel excited; it is our respect towards him. Drumming makes our King feel pride, and when he feels pride, then he becomes more supportive to our community.

Well, I think I need to get up and get ready to socialise at the Chief's palace. We always have issues to discuss or to sort out, sometimes from the palace or from the councillor

(Ba'ale), or from the community of the hunters. I do not want to go early this time, except if he, himself, sends for me – that is the Chief. In fact, I need to spend more time inside today because of the stews I cooked yesterday. I need to warm them up and eat at home, else I will have to throw them away. I have got so many foods at home. The whole house smells so much of meat, as if it is the (alapata) market. I think I will take time before I go to the Chief's place, probably around evening time.

***

Chapter Three

"At Chief Hunter's House"
Little Hunter

Four colleagues of hunting came to pay the Chief a visit. They were standing side by side. Then, altogether and in time with one another they moved to the right and then to the left, then they walked straight to the Chief, according to our greeting tradition. This was to show that no evil was hidden in your heart. When you are given this sort of greeting, the Chief Hunter could suddenly shake your hand or use his chest to hit your own. In most cases, he chested me, and I mostly fell down. Sometimes I do not like him chesting me. But we hunters are accustomed to it. Guest, visitors or strangers usually find it funny and burst out laughing. Well, it does not matter, I shrugged to myself. That is our culture; you cannot change it, you have got to get used to it.

This time he did not chest me; instead, he drew out his left hand and we shook up, shook down, then drew out our hands whilst clenching each other's fingers, and kissed the tip of the hand we shook. That was an unexpected warm greeting from Chief. One of the hunters sitting on the bench then dragged his bum to the right and created a position for me to sit. Another hunter said, "Chief must know you very well."

"Yes," I replied, "a pleasant man who loves us all."

"Yes, ho yes. You would not believe this; he knew every one of us and treated us accordingly. He is remarkably good," the man expressed, "my prayer is this time next year God should provide him a child!"

I replied, "May Ogun (God) accept this." Our conversation prompted me to look into the face of the man and become more familiar with him, but the man was too difficult to look at. I tried to look at him straight in the eyes, but my eyes refused to stay on him for more than two seconds. I looked again, I gazed at him from the face to the toes. He was slim, about 5ft 9ins tall and his mouth was fully soaked in kola nut. His breath was that of kola, the tobacco that he smoked had definitely made his teeth black. His teeth were much worse than mine. Then the enjoyment began.

Chief Hunter rang his bells as usual and said to the servant, "Can you please bring two kegs of palm wine (emu), one for that side and the second to that side." Then he turned to me and said, "I will likely speak with you later, because I will have to finish the response to the message from our Majesty the King Ilodi II." Later, another four people joined our meeting.

"Why so many people?" I asked faintly, forgetting that I was not alone.

Then this wicked-looking hunter heard me and said, "Have you forgotten that today is an important day, a day that we celebrate the Chief Hunter, because like the King he makes you content, they use their wealth to support and respond to the community. Did you not learn how great this community is, after all this time?"

Silently, inside me, I felt cold, then I blurted out, "Should that be the case, how come I have not found myself a girlfriend or someone special to marry me?"

The wicked-faced hunter responded, "Getting a wife is not easy, you do not need one. As for me, I regret marrying, you know. I will advise you now and assure you, you do not need a wife."

I turned my head to the right, and my eyes went straight out of the window to the sky as if somebody was there to respond to what I had just heard. The Chief called, "Little –" but before he could finish saying Hunter, I answered him. He asked me to come and sit down beside him. "Any problem?" I asked.

"No problem, I just want you by my side," Chief muttered.

"Just a minute," I replied, then I went back to my original seat and told the four hunters that I was going to sit with Chief.

"No problem," they all said. But the wicked one emphasised, "Remember, you don't need it."

The Chief asked me, "What you don't need?"

"Chief, I will talk to you later about this issue."

The Deputy then jokingly said to me, "You are becoming too popular, Little!"

"Thank you," I said to the Deputy.

"When are you going to get married?" he asked.

"Wife, I don't even have girlfriend. It's not easy to marry!" I said.

Then the Chief said, "Only God can predict who will marry. You know, not every man will marry. Likewise, not every man that marries will have children!" and everyone burst out laughing. But when I took a look around, you could figure out that not everyone took it as a joke. The Deputy who sat close to me responded to the speech with irate eyes that depicted disgust and violence. I could not utter a word, I kept my mouth shut, and I concluded that I didn't like the rowdiness Chief caused.

"No one asked you to join this conversation, Big Hunter," retorted the Deputy to Chief Hunter. "And you should not be sarcastic, because only God can provide a child. We often hear of people that get a child through this and that, like worshipping water, an idol, elephant. But if we are focused in our prayer to God for a child, you will be surprised. The type of child you will get would be a non-problematic child. And that type of child God will provide you, Chief Hunter. Everybody say amen!"

We all chimed in with, "Aaaaaaaaaaaamen!"

The Deputy continued to pray, "This time next year, your wife will be pregnant and you will rear the child, amen."

Again, everybody said, "Aaaaaamen," except for the Chief Hunter, who murmured, "So, you say every year, when you have drunk and enjoyed yourselves. I am sick and tired of your prayers!"

"Who is muttering?" asked Deputy.

"I said so you say every year. When you people enjoy yourself to the maximum, you started praying. Prayer that has no meaning, no gratification, and no enthusiasm," repeated Chief.

"Quiet!" the Deputy Hunter's voice echoed around and shook the room. The whole place came to an abrupt silence. The two heads were facing each other squarely. Deputy continued, "As I vividly believe there is a 'GOD', this time next year we are going to celebrate the Hunters festival with your family and a son of yours running around here." Then, we said "Aaaaaaaaaaaamen!" again. "If truly you are the God that created heaven and earth, and you created Di and Tes and they joined together as husband and wife, and because I, Ti, speaking and praying from the bottom of my heart, pray that this couple be blessed with a child this time next year. I say this prayer through our God Ogun."

"Aaaaaaaaaaaamen."

"Everyone has had too much to drink," said Chief Hunter.

Yet we all continued, "So it shall be. So it shall be for you, because we all love you."

"I promise you all that should that be the case, you will all taste the big cat stew, if your wishes come true. *I repeat this.* You will all taste and eat *THE TIGER meat and stew* on our next festival's annual dance, if it comes to be true as you all said," said Chief Hunter before he sat down.

Then one of the hunters rose up and said, "Chief, your promise is fake, a fallacy. I don't doubt you but it not as easy to kill a lion or tiger."

"Why?" someone amongst them asked.

"The animal is too elusive and strong to kill. You can only kill him if you are in a team. For one person, I think it is too difficult to kill. You may think you see a tiger now in the bush, but within a fraction of a second, he has disappeared, and if care is not taken, he will kill you first. At times it is as if the animal knows you are hunting for him and therefore you may not see him at all!" said the hunter. Some of hunters looked at him with disbelief; they seemed to be overexcited with the thought of tasting a tiger.

Our meeting then focused on tiger stews. Everybody was asking each other whether they had tasted tiger before. It

26

seemed that only I, Chief Hunter and the Deputy had tasted it. Therefore, everyone wanted the prayer to come true.

***

Chapter Four

Rumours had spread to the King's palace. Some unscrupulous people had said there was a big fight at yesterday's meeting at Chief Hunter's place. The King when made aware of this issue, paused and waited on the call of Chief Hunter. When he had received no contact, he sent a messenger to visit the Chief Hunter to ask about the meeting of yesterday and why there was a fight.

The messenger took the direct route to the Chief Hunter's house. The door to his house was wide open. The messenger knocked three times. "You are welcome, please come in," Tes replied to the knock. He entered, and she quickly got up from her seat and half kneeled down to greet the King's messenger. The messenger laid down for her halfway, as she was the wife of Chief Hunter, who was absent. These gestures were signs of respect. "Where is big hunter?" he asked.

"He surely went to the bush. He always likes that," she replied.

"How soon will he be back?"

"I really don't know, maybe a day or two!"

"The King heard there was a problem here last night with some people fighting? Is it true or false? Surely there is no problem!"

"Problem? There are no known problems."

"There were rumours in the palace that a big fight erupted here last night."

"Although there was an argument, my husband dealt with it."

"No problems at all then? The King was so worried."

"Please tell the King there are no problems at all. The entire event was all right and there was no trouble at all."

"I believe you. I will inform the King. Rest assured that there is no problem at all," he replied.

On that she went and opened the calabash where they kept kola nuts and brought out two kola nuts and gave them to the messenger. "Thank you very much," he said and went out. "Bye for now!"

"My regards to the King and the palace!"

"Thank you, bye!"

The messenger reached the palace and gave the message to the King accordingly. The King replied, "I thought as much. If there was any problem, he would have come in immediately after the meeting; he is known for that." The King was sitting with his political left and political right chiefs, who seemed to have been aware about the problems at Chief Hunter's place and were discussing among themselves. They discussed how the Chief Hunter would celebrate next year's festival with a big cat stew. The lefties admitted that Chief Hunter was going to celebrate it with tiger stew. "Ha ha ha ha!" the King laughed and every one of them stopped and paid attention. "Is that what you heard, left? Is that what you heard, right?'

"Yes, Your Majesty. Certainly yes, Your Majesty," one of them replied.

Another one said, "It's high time our King should wear tiger skin, which symbolise power and honour of this town."

"Certainly yes!" everyone said, including the King. "And the leg of the cat must come to the palace," they all laughed with good humour. Then the King relieved them all by retreating in to the inner rooms of the palace.

There were gossips passing around the palace about Chief Hunter and his family. One person said his wife Tes seemed to be a nice woman. She had apparently knelt abruptly with her forehead touching the ground when greeting a right chief. She was complimented by the chief for such manners. Another said she must have come from a good home, not like girls you find in the houses of the left chiefs. A lot of those girls do not have education; they hardly even knew how to greet a person! Suddenly, as soon as the Olori Aafin, the King's wife, stepped in to the room with her first leg, they all went silent.

What was unknown to them all was that Tes came from the palace. She was a relative of the King.

***

Chapter Five

Chief Hunter's Wife, Tes

"This is the contemplation of a good season for every one of us," said Chief Hunter.

"What does that mean?" asked one of his subordinates, who was listening to him.

"I can see it and I can feel it. This period is going to be good and all our undertakings, our wants would be fulfilled with joy," Chief Hunter replied.

Very early in the morning, he woke up and got dressed up. Normally, he would not wake me up unless it was essential for him to do so. But I always wake up anytime he wakes, and I pretend as if I don't awake. Looking at the sky, it was midnight when he opened the door gently and shut it behind him. You would hardly know someone left the house or entered. My husband is really an artful dodger. His footsteps never make a sound; he's always behind you without you knowing. However, I knew he had left the house to go to the bush and at the hut there he would stay.

On the bed I rolled to the left and to the right, I could not get my sleep again. I tried. I closed my eyes to sleep, but I could not. I rolled down to his pillow's side and sniffed his pillow. *He had only just left, but I was missing my husband*, I thought to myself and it is not really the morning, or else I should start cleaning the house.

Suddenly, I opened my eyes and it was morning.

***

Chapter Six

Chief Hunter

In the bush, I began singing one of my usual songs. When I'm idle, I sing. These were songs sung by our forefathers which go like this: *Ero Ilu Ojeje ojeje e ba mi ki baba mi ojeje wipe eran to fi sile o ojeje orogun ma mu je isu ewura to gan gogo ojeje lorogun ma fun mi je ojeje.* This I sung repeatedly.

The sky suddenly changed colour, I reckoned it was going to rain. I needed to skilfully cover myself because during the rain some animals become slower. This is a great opportunity to get some kill. Just a moment ago, I'd seen a big beast with mighty calves. These beasts have big heads, the size of a buffalo but with a smaller horn, they were not so tall, and their skin was woolly. They are very dangerous to kill, and I don't want to start my day with the beast that could be hunting me both night and day. Carefully, I looked up the tree right in front of me and checked in case there was a snake, tiger, leopard or cheetah living up there. It was empty, so I climbed this tree. "Very good," I said to myself, "now I am at the centre for seeing every species which I could not see before!"

I was especially looking for the animals a bit further down, not too far from the river. The antelopes. I could see that two of them were fighting for dominance over the females. I came down the tree, walked about 500 paces away and climbed another adjacent tree in the area. I brought out my double barrel, which I inherited from my father, and shot one of the fighting antelopes by their armpit. Then the rest started to run away. Whilst the beasts were still running, I went and took the kill. I covered it up with banana leaves. Quickly, I shot another one; it still tried to run, so I shot it again. Then I took both kills and brought them into one my old huts in the bush. It was time for a break. I rummaged and took a kola nut out and ate it. This helped to prevent me from sleeping until I wanted to.

I'll take a nap now.

I was awakened by the roar of the big cat. It was the male lion that answered to my whispering the last month I hunted here. My instinct told me it was a friend. So, I went not too far from my hut and got myself a kill. A gazelle this time. Then I looked around to try and find the big cat. I saw him; he was about half a mile away to where I was down the stream. He could see me. I dropped the kill and climbed to the top of the tree. Within a short time, he came around for the kill, and stood there and ate.

I made my way back to the hut, and I could see that the sun was trying to come out to brighten the day. A quick glance at adaba (dove), it was approximately the fifth hour in the morning, so I took the rest of the kill and headed home.

***

Chapter Seven

Chief Hunter

The journey home took me almost two hours or more. I went straight into the shed made as a bathroom and had a good wash of my body. Without disturbing her, I entered our bed. She was fast and sound asleep. I moved very close to her, with her bum very, very close to my waist. My body came to a quick and sudden erection. I believed she was having a similar feeling. I felt her tenderly stroke her right hand on my penis, though not opening her eyes. She reciprocated my feeling and her mouth locked on to mine. It was a good session that went on for so long that I discharged twice into her body. We could not clean up ourselves, as we slept again in each other's arms.

We woke up at eleventh hour. "Can you make me some herb tea?" I asked.

"And, would you like to eat something?" she asked back.

"No, I would be all right with the tea and bring my tobacco pipe."

"Wow! My husband," she said.

"Yes?" I replied.

"I love you; you must have enjoyed that?"

"Very much, I love you."

"Thank you."

"When you are ready, there are two antelopes I killed last night, if you could look after them for me."

"That is the way you are! I will always love you!" she continued, "Hayyyyye! How do you manage to bring them home?"

"Well, I carried them on my shoulder."

"You are lovely, lovely and lovely!" She came back to the bed and gave me a hug. I held her down, slowly put her back into the bed and gently removed her towel from her body and held her two beautiful breasts with my hand. I put one of the breasts into my mouth gently and went into her underpants and gently stroked my erect penis into her vagina. The session was not long, and I found myself back sleeping again.

It was a sweet erection, hunger and thirst for sex that actually woke me. Still half asleep, I used my right hand to stroke the pillow; I felt no sign of her on the bed with me. I shouted her name and that she should come in right now. She rushed in as if something had happened to me. "Please sleep with me, I felt lonely," I moaned to her.

"I am too busy out there, I thought something wrong had happened that is why I rushed in. Obviously, you are all right, see yourself," she replied. Then she giggled and smiled, the smile that I usually fell in love with. This made my erection stronger and we rolled down on each other so tight that you could hardly know that there were two people on the bed until she raised her head up and began to suffocate me with excited kisses.

I went to the bath shed and got water to rinse my mouth. I gurgled with cold water and had a quick shower. This made me feel good. "Your food is at the table," she said.

"You need to see me eat, even though you are not eating," I responded.

"I won't be long at all," she replied and within a few minutes she joined me on the dining table. "The King was here," she said.

"Of course, I knew he must have sent one of his messengers to me with an errand, why?" I asked.

"People went to tell him there was fight at the meeting held four days ago," she replied.

"Well, he will know there is no problem, I'm sure," I said in response, "and this hairdo of yours makes you look gorgeous and presentable and it actually adds more to your beauty."

"Thank you, mine well-luck," she replied with a gentle smile. She cut a piece of yam with meat and put it in my mouth.

"All this shows the affection you have for me," I said with enthusiasm and I reciprocated with the same action. "I must let you know that one of the legs of the antelope must go to the palace," I said.

"For your information, so far the total money we made from the last meat sold in the market was a total 2,402 cowries and the contribution received so far from the drinking donations was total 320 cowries. Sooner or later when I am finished with this, I will ask my sister to take them to the market. I reckon this would fetch roughly 1,000 to 1,250 cowries," she replied to me.

"When we get that money, we shall take them to the King and purchase some gold. You see the donation we received is yours to keep and spend to make you look more beautiful for me," I said.

She stood up and then knelt down in appreciation for the gift of money. "Mine well-luck, I think it would be necessary for me to visit the Little Hunter. It has been a while. I would like me and my sister to pay him a visit."

"Yes, yes, ho yes of course, including me I think all of us should go and spend time with him. How do we know whether he is in or not?"

"When Siha, my cousin's sister, was coming from the market she saw him in the market, so definitely he must be indoors."

"Have you been sending her to him?"

"No, they don't even know each other."

"But you just said she saw him."

"The Deputy Hunter's daughter pointed to her one time that, that is the Little Hunter."

"That is okay," I finally said.

***

Little Hunter

Tonight, I must go out there and see some of my traps, they might have caught some animals. I would not know until I have a look. Some hooks might have gone because of the time that had passed, likewise I must prepare to spend some days out there because there are some crops which I may need to bring to the market, and my maize farm may need to be harvested and I may possibly plant some of my tomato's pots in between the maize fields.

So, I gathered my gear together and headed to the farm, whilst hunting along the way. Before I reached my hut, there were about five traps I checked. The first one caught a rodent still alive, and I used my kumo, a small rod, gently on its head and put it in my bag. The second was empty, still the same as I kept it, the third was also the same. The fourth one had caught a little rat which was dead and rotten and the last one had caught a guinea fowl. I was very excited because live guinea fowl are more expensive than the dead ones. Therefore, I found a piece of leaf and covered her head and tied the two legs together and then I went straight to one of my hut in the bush for bit of comfort and rest until it started to rain.

I could not do much again and I slept. I was awakened by the cockerel crow. My journey home will take me two hours. I headed home through the market so that I could sell the guinea fowl. Sold. Job well done. I came back home and planned for another time to go back to the farm.

Since most of my time spent inside at home is for sleeping, sometimes I have to create a job for myself to escape the boredom. People don't come often to me. I don't have many friends out there, the only place I socialise at is Chief Hunter's. The rest of people I know are older than me and they don't go out or perhaps they go out and only my house escapes their mind when they are passing through. I don't know. I made a fire to cook the rodent which I killed, when all of a sudden, I got a knock on my door.

Whoa, what a pleasant surprise, Chief! "I love it!" I shouted.

"I've been thinking when I should give you a surprise visit with my family," Chief Hunter replied with a smile.

"Great, great, Chief! I love visitors, it has been a long time ago since I have enjoyed that. Perhaps, it was last when my pa was alive," I responded.

"May his soul rest in perfect peace," said the young lady with Tes and Chief Hunter.

"Thank you. And who are you?" I asked.

"This is my wife's younger cousin, Siha, she came to visit us from the village," replied Chief Hunter.

Our eyes met; the lady had no expression. I shivered then found courage to say. "Is a great pleasure to meet you"

Everyone sat down on the mat laid on the living room floor. Except Chief, who sat on the slipper's chair. This made you look down on those below you as if you are a school teacher in the classroom. "For the first time in my life, I've had a good use of this chair. It was erected there, is unmoveable, definitely serving a purpose," I said.

Chief Hunter replied, "Yes, everyone always erects it in their home because of visitors, such as the King. It is for *very important visitors* that could visit at any time of the day. They must be comfortable. This shows how you welcome dignitaries in your home, and dignitaries themselves knew whom they visit amongst the communities." We all burst into laughter. "It is true, be quiet," he said to us. We were silent; moreover, he was among the dignitaries he was mentioning about. In fact, I do not know why we laughed.

As I dashed away to the kitchen, Chief Hunter's wife was right behind me and I was glad. I grabbed the old Scotch whisky, gave it to her, with myself carrying the little table, and followed her to the living room. The whisky had been there since the death of my dad, 20 years ago. I don't know what it tasted like, but I quite believe it's a strong alcoholic drink like our homemade rum, 'Ogogoro'. I had the occasional drink of this, especially when I felt cold or had a toothache. Well, just like our tradition says, he who brings drink brings happiness, he who brings kola nuts brings joy, he who brings honey brings gladness and he who brings water brings in life.

Chief Hunter started to pray and every one of us was saying 'Ase', meaning Amen, to every prayer he made. He came to his old prayer that this time next year, I would be served here by a woman that would be my wife. My Ase was a bit quiet. Only one person said amen and that was his wife, he continued to pray with such wild emotion and only concluded when we all said Ase. He had a sip of the whisky and passed it around. It tasted very nice and very, very hot when swallowing it. That is an imported drink for you anyway.

I made my way to the kitchen and all of a sudden, the Chief's wife was with me. "What are you cooking?" she asked. "Since you are around now, I think I would need to cook something filling for all of us," I said.

"Well, you can go and join your friend in the living room, but you must call my cousin to come and help me do the cooking," she replied. Her sister did not wait for my call; she was already on her way to the kitchen. She must have heard us discussing or it was a coincidence. "Your sis wants you," I said. She shrugged as if she was deaf and dumb. I developed total hatred towards her, there was no good gesture in her at all. *I don't like her*, I thought repeatedly in my mind before I approached Chief Hunter.

"Little Hunter, I would like to show you some things. It is an uneasy head that wears a crown. My wife is different to

41

Mine wife. Mine wife is the wife you believe is yours and nobody else; no one can talk to her, she's your possession. In fact, you don't even want to see anyone with her. The woman herself does not feel free; gradually, she loses her love, comfort, and trust in you. Your security and protection mean nothing as she is now fighting for herself and her safety would be the best way out.

"But '*My Wife*' is not a one-sided love; it is both sides in love with one another. That is why I pray that God should give you your wife. If you married your wife, you will be rich in wealth, security, knowledge and be comfortable. With your love, you have security, protection and gladness; moreover, there are blessing from the Almighty. That is happiness..." Chief trailed on. Chief Hunter was not actually finished when I heard a knock on the door. "Was you expecting someone?" Chief asked.

"No," I replied. I went to the door and opened it. It was my father's family friend. As soon as I opened the door, he started talking as usual and gave me a hug.

"I can hear the Chief Hunter voice," he said.

"Yes, exactly he is around to say hello as well," I replied. "It's the Chief Priest," I shouted back at the others.

They both danced and sang our special greeting song of hunters and shook each other's hands and hugged. "This was a pleasant surprise, it's been a long time since I last saw you," Chief Hunter said.

"So, you knew Tad?" I asked.

"Of course, yes," replied Tad himself.

"In this area we are one, we all knew each other," added Chief Hunter. "Except those ones we are not happy with, thief or stranger thief. And they know themselves, and when we

42

find them, what do we do to them? We burn them and burn all their property and belongings down to ashes," continued Chief Hunter.

"There are two things we oppose in this village," I said, "that is theft and the witchcraft that kills children."

"Exactly!" responded both Chief and Tad.

"This is my wife Tes," Chief said.

"I am pleased to meet you," Tad said to Tes and addressing Chief, he continued, "well, the first time I knew her was at your wedding, although that was too busy to know someone." She greeted him by kneeling down on both legs and Tad started to pray for her, "No evil or devil will take you out of your home. Your home with Chief will be smooth with honey, wealth, joy and gladness. With good time and peace will God give you a child. God will give you a pleasant child that worthy and not just a child." We all responded with, "Amen".

Si, Tes' cousin, knelt down beside her while the prayer was going on; seeing this, Tad switched the prayer to Si. "A good husband God will provide for you. Husband that will look after you, protect you and comfort you, God will provide for you. When you will meet him, God will give you the thought and knowledge to admire him." Again, we chimed in with, "Amen."

"Please rise up, get up my princesses," Tad requested. They rose up on to their feet, and Si went back to the kitchen.

Tes went to her husband and whispered to his right ear. All we could see was that Chief held her head gently and moved her head forward to his head and the two mouths joined each other. What were they doing? "Is that kissing?" I asked abruptly.

"Yes," Tad said.

"I am now learning," I responded. I stood there motionless, watching; this is what love does to people. Isn't it enjoyable? I asked myself. Of course, the actions of animals are also the actions of humans. If you have been to the bush and on top of the tree, you will see and be bemused at how animals behave in their dwellings. As well you will know there is no difference between human and animals, even the birds. I was enjoying their company indeed, until Si came and touched me by the shoulder where I stood, to inform me that the food was ready.

"Tell your sister," I said.

She went straight to her cousin who was on the husband's lap and said, "The food is now ready for serving, OK."

"OK, thank you. I almost forgot about it," said Tes and she got up quickly and they both dashed off to the kitchen.

We now came to one large room where all of us sat and had a quiet dinner. In fact, it was long time I have had to sit in this area of the house – since the death of my dad. You may ask me, why it is always since the death of my dad? It is simply because my mum died before him, this was immediately after my birth. So, I do not know my mum. My father brought me up with my grandmother, who died when I was seven years old.

The dinner table was rich with fruits and with different types of fried meats and sweet corn, all in separate bowls. The first meat bowl contained the pure meat of antelope, which was roasted with chilli pepper and onion; the second one was guinea fowl grilled with pure palm oil and pepper and curry, which made it so delicious. The third bowl of meat contained assorted cat meat mixed with onion and tomatoes slices, and it was chopped small, so it could simply be eaten while you were socialising with a glass of natural palm wine *(emu and oguro)*. The last bowl was an appetiser. It was a boiled watery juice, seasoned with curry, onion and pepper. It was meant to open your bowel so that you could be able to eat as much as possible, and if you were already eating, you would be able to eat more. You would pass gas out easily, both from your mouth and from the bottom. There was a big white bowl, this contained pounded yam. As you opened it, you could see the lid was sweating.

The Chief Hunter sat on the high table facing Tes. Si sat at the left side of her cousin and Tad sat facing me. The table was a six-chair dining table. We started to eat, and then the Chief reminded me about praying. He prayed, "Bless this food ho God and bless those who are starving, feed them ho God."

"Amen."

"I like this prayer so much and I got it from the Priest," Chief Hunter said.

"From me, that was a good prayer," Tad responded.

"Priest, I'm lonely and need someone very close to my heart," I confided in Tad.

"Don't be too hasty, God's time is the best. Therefore, whenever we say pray a prayer that actually touches your emotions, your feelings, never feel reluctant to say amen. You can never tell when the angels of God are passing or sitting among us. Whatever we say, they take it and accept it, and so shall it be," Tad responded.

"Thank you very much," I sighed.

"This is a delicious dinner," Chief said.

"Quite delicious," the Priest and I responded.

"This is how I used to enjoy myself when I pay visits to Chief," I boasted. "Tes, she always takes good care of me and several times she would give me some food to take away home. That is the way she is since we were very small."

"Only God can thank you, Chief Priest, because the blessing of today is yours," Chief said to the Priest.

We all ate, every one of us ate and filled up. Si cleared the table, she wiped it down neatly. Yet all of that did not make any significant impact on my opinion about her, because I believe my future wife would be someone who would be loyal, lovable, and chatty and would be like my mother. As my father used to describe her, my mother was loveable; she was a respectful and honest woman that could give any part of her body for your safety. That is the type of woman I want, an honest woman.

I could see that everyone ate, and the tired Priest and Chief Hunter were dozing off. Tes was leaning on her husband's arm. I guess you could say everyone was now eager to go home. I told Priest to wait behind and keep my company. That was okay, he said. While Chief Hunter was attempting to go, he started praying, as was customary, to bless our travels here and there.

They've all gone, and I have to do quickly now before it's too late for me to go for hunting.

***

Chapter Eight

Little Hunter

Hunting and farming are my business, I thought. When people see you at home on a Monday morning, the first thing they ask is, "Are you all right? I hope you feel well today." Then, they gossip to your next-door neighbour, "I saw your neighbour, he did not go out. Hope his feeling all right, is there any problem that you noticed?" Their small talk could take hours, until you came out and defended yourself. Sometimes, people do not mind their business; they liked to poke their nose into your affairs. We call this poke-nose. They cannot help you in trouble but just mocking you and laughing at you is their business.

Without hesitation, I got all my gear together. My headlight was full of palm oil; no amount of rain would switch it off. My hand light also was fantastically full up, as if I had not used them for ages. I pulled up my bante, a sort of miniskirt and gathered my long and short rods. I remembered I have to take ounde and ifunpa, my waist and arm weapons bands. For hunting these are important, especially when I know I am going to spend a fortnight in the bush. Some of these ounde and ifunpa belonged to my dad. I knew what they were used for and how you could wake them up and start them working as normal. The ounde and ifunpa are medicine to which special incantations must be spoken, so that they can respond to the use. These weapons have different forms, my ounde and ifunpa may not look the same as Chief Hunters own. Without wasting much time, I put them on. I felt them heavy on my waist up to my belly. Yes, yes, yes. I feel them as if they were talking to me. Gently, gently, I thought. I rubbed them, on my waist and arm, with guinea pepper, which I had ground in my mouth with a mixture of saliva. I felt a sudden relief and I moved on my way. If do not browse around or do any other things, the journey is two hours, so I decided to go there directly. The journey wasn't too long; of course, it was not. I am getting too fast with everything I do these days. Well, I am not getting smaller but bigger, even my age.

In the farm, I took a look at the surroundings, everything seemed all right, except the maize plantations, which of course were damaged by goats. Then I realised that it was elephants that damaged the plantation, the footmarks showed it all and their puddles. And one of my farm walls went with them as well. "Were they still around?" I asked silently. I followed their footsteps until I found myself in another territory, but they could not be seen. Then I backed off and returned to my farm. I felt like having a cold shower before I went to bed. I dashed around at the water tank place. It was emptied and dry. "Why? Why? Why?" I groaned. I searched my sack I got my bottle out that was full of water, I drank some and used a small amount of it to wash my face down before I went to bed. Food. No, I don't need any food, the journey and all the trouble had filled me up.

I could not stop thinking about how the tank was empty while lying on my bed, until a thought came to my head that it could be the elephant that emptied the tank. In the morning, I should check carefully. Of course, elephants could be outside and drink your tank empty and if it is a mud tank, you will be lucky if it is not broken. I woke up, it was the morning and it was the cock's crow that woke me up. I went to take a good look at the tank to see whether it was leaking. But there was nothing. Surely, it was the elephant that damaged the plantations and that emptied the tank. Then a thought came to my head, I knew them. This group is not big, but rather they are mini elephants, as we call them. They are bad, destructible and fierce fighters. When you see them, be careful and do not run; if you are running stop and start to walk. See their reaction before you continue what you are doing; however, if possible, change your vicinity.

I started the day's work repairing the damages. I re-erected the damaged roof and put in a wall. To fill up the tank would be an evening job, I thought. I am yet to have breakfast, let alone lunch. I did not let any evil thoughts take up my mind space, I continued with my job. It took me ten good journeys to and from the river to fill up the tank. After, I took one little yam and a leg of antelope, mixed it with onions, red pepper, a little peanut oil and tomatoes. As soon as I finished eating, nothing was left than to sleep. Quickly, I remembered a bottle of palm wine was on the rack. I drank it down.

On my bed I thought, not until harvest time will I know whether all my effort and performance were outstanding or not. That was the time people went around buying farm products, fruits and assorted meats with different flavours. I need to get myself ready for hunting because I do not have much meat to sell. My customers would be disappointed if they have not got much to buy from me.

It's been a while since I've gone for daylight hunting; nothing wrong with it, only you may not get much to kill as compared to hunting at night. Even though it's daylight hunting, you will need to get all your gadgets prepared for any eventuality because it may be a deadly night

I was headed to my destination, which was adjacent to the rainforest. I had not walked too far down before I saw the first animal. But it wasn't impressive at all, could you guess? It was the poor old man called Tortoise. In fact, we hunters dislike tortoises on our journey to work or from work. Seeing a tortoise means do not hunt, you might as well return home or else all your effort for that day may not yield any fruitful responses, so I was told. It has never happened to me, but I could vividly remember, my dad said, "A tortoise would talk to you, depending on your state of mind." As I was trying to take my eyes off him, I heard someone say, "Little Hunter, would you ignore me? How would you say you did not see me, as big as I am?" This conversation isn't real; I am not going to be stupid, hearing voices when there is no one to talk to. I picked the tortoise and put it in my sack by my left side, but instinct told me you need to kill it else; you would be disturbed for the whole journey. By the side of a big tree in front of me, I saw a big stone. Before it could make a noise, I rolled the sack bag and suddenly I smashed it with the stone. The blood was too much, of course. I've always wanted that sack to be blood-soaked and dried. Therefore, I rolled the sack so that the blood did not drain away without being used. I needed it to be dry, else all my clothes and body would be blood-stained.

Some moments after that I could not cope with what I was seeing. The forest became an illusion, as though I was living in a wonderland. I was not day dreaming. Then I saw her, a pretty lady come, out of the footpath. She was talking or singing to herself; she didn't see me or was aware of me. I became so frightened. I felt I should go home, as there was one thing with hunting: you must not be frightened or scared. You must be completely strong and hard like a stone or else you would be crushed down like an insect. Quickly, I got my composure back.

I thought, perhaps she is playing hide and seek with me. Then she disappeared and in another few seconds, she reappeared about a mile's distance away from me. It's as if she is watching me, it's scaring me. I did not want to tangle with what I do not know. I decided that I should be heading home, enough is enough. As I was walking, my head was getting heavy as if it was going to burst. I said I must be very quick now before I break down and I am unable to move or walk. I tried not to raise my blood's pressure; however, I could not help it because I started shiver with cold and my leg became stiffer. Yes, I could hear the sound that something was coming behind me, the smell was so disgusting. I have to kill it, I thought; yet, if it does no harm, let it live.

The memory of smashing the tortoise head keeps haunting me. I struggled on. I needed to go and see the Chief Hunter; he was the only one to get me out of this problem.

Later and in my sleep, I realised you must not kill a tortoise like that. I promised never to do again.

***

Chapter Nine

Chief Hunter

This is not funny at all! "I, the Chief Hunter," I said to myself, "I hardly see some animals that I can boast of killing!" So far all I have been seeing are reptiles. Where have all the animals gone to? I'm in the wrong place. NO! Everything just doesn't seem to work in my favour. It's three days now that I left Tes at home, in the town, and two and half days since I left my farm, and I have not killed a rat! I better go back to my farm and feed the chicken and the rams. I'll check my traps; I may be lucky. I didn't even know I was this far away.

It is obvious that you sometimes know you are not alone in the bush. Whenever this happens, that is how you know you are not alone. If my mind is not too troubled, then I won't be afraid and I can just continue with my business. Whenever the mind is too much troubled, your life is in danger of being a dinner for one unscrupulous animal, like a wolf, bear, gorilla or tiger.

My traps caught some guinea fowls, I slaughtered them and put them in my sack, and I carried the yam with my bicycle trailer. As I was heading home towards the town, it was getting dark and I could feel the fresh air of evening.

I saw my wife, who was so happy. "You have missed me?" I asked.

"Yes!" she replied.

"I am happy now," I told her, then I bent my head down. She started to smell my hair down to my neck and her mouth found my mouth gently and I kissed her. "Please let me get to the bath," I said. She replied, "No," gently. So, I carried her to the bathroom and we had a romantic shower that I'd never had before.

"I have cooked one of your favourite dishes," she said excitedly.

"Would you please bring it?" I asked.

"Of course."

"I am starving, I haven't eaten anything this morning," I replied. She dashed off to the kitchen instantly. "Whoa, whoa you haven't touched or eaten out of it?" I asked surprised.

"Yes darling, I have been too busy to eat; moreover, I have been thinking about you, to feel you and eat you. That made me cook your favourite dish, 'asaro' porridge made with plantain, fried fish, not dry but moist and subtle."

We both sat and ate. In fact, she is a good cook. "Delicious!" I said, and she put a spoonful in my mouth. I could see the love brewing and growing in both of us. As soon as we finished the food, she was so tired, and I laid down with her. I thought about how fragile she was, she was the centre of my life. People used to say of our tribe, the men come first and there's no dignity for women. Pure lies! There is nothing different between them and those of other lands, only the respect we have and owe to each other. You must respect the husband, as it is in the Bible and as is part of our custom too.

"Chief…"

"Yes, love."

"When is it your anniversary? Can you remind me again?"

I looked at the calendar on the wall. "Wahoo, Wahoo is getting close and looming, in October," I responded.

"I have been noticing that you have not been bringing some of the animals you used to bring therefore, our stock of meat has not been increasing so far. Is there any problem?" she then asked.

Good wife, I am glad I have got someone to share my opinion with, I thought to myself. I found it very interesting how I could discuss my problems with her. "Darling, do you know, I have not been seeing some animals like I used to in the past. Reptiles and fowls have become my favourites, I do not know why!" I exclaimed.

"Why?" she asked.

"I have killed leopard and cheetah before but nowadays nothing at all," I told her.

"Should I come hunting with you?" she asked sweetly.

"That would be when I am not going too far from the farm. It is not good for you to follow me to the bush when you know nothing of hunting. You can stay in the farm and watch, but you must promise to do whatever I say," I responded.

"Yes, I promise," she said.

"My panic is not because I could not get any animals, but for the vows which I have committed myself to. Would this situation change? Yes, of course, it could change. My instincts tell me that during the summertime, animals move from dry land to a fresh area where the leaves and plants are fresh, where they can find delicious food to eat. You see, animals are like human beings. Perhaps, I should hunt nearer the rainforest."

"Yes, you are right, darling"

"I have tried but I keep getting the animals we hunters dislike, reptiles".

"Well, you still get something, never mind for what you don't get," she concluded. I started to worry, when the hunters come, as they do every year to drink, eat and dance, there will be no proper meat. Yet, how can they ask me for what I did not provide or tiger pepper soup, or dinner, when my wife is still not pregnant. She overheard my murmuring and walked to me briskly and said, "Darling, don't worry, why do you put too much load on your shoulders? Leave everything to God." As she focused on me, I suddenly felt aroused. I could see the glittering beauty in her radiant eyes. "Let us take a walk," she said. I declined.

"Let us do this my own way," I responded. I stepped forward, put my right hand behind her neck and used the left hand to move her forward, then my mouth found hers. I lifted her totally off the ground and took her to the bed.

This time it was different because she thrust her hand inside my pants and got a hold of my penis, which was as strong as a wooden stick. She undressed me. She was on the top and I could see her two nipples were very hard. I gently put both hands on top of the breasts and squeezed both of them at the same time. When I entered her, she responded gently, "I love you so much; do not leave me, you are made for me."

"I have run your bath, darling, please come on down, I don't want it to get cold!" she said.

I got my bath robe (usually white cloth), so I walked to the bath. "I need more hot water," I said.

"That is why I want you quickly in the bath!"

She didn't know that I intentionally wanted her to come and have a bath with me. As she dropped the water in, it was too hot, yet I couldn't resist. I suddenly pulled her straight into the bath. "Ho no no, I already had bath before," she said. Before she could continue speaking, my lips covered hers. I was erect again and we started to have sex. Yet we managed not to overdo it, you know they say whenever you are trying for a baby, be careful not to overdo it, or else the baby would not come. To get a baby, you should not have sex every day.

We dressed up and took a stroll to the market.

"It's been a long time since people have seen us together!"

"I love your dress".

"Thank you, it's one of the dresses you bought me for my birthday."

"How beautiful you look in it!"

"I love you."

"Should I take that as a thank you?"

"As you feel!"

"Oh really!"

She giggled and then said, "Thank you, I will always love you." She tried to kiss me, so I bent down. We reached the oak tree, and I said we should sit and take some fresh air. As we sat down, I looked at her face while she was staring at me.

"You love to stare at me a lot!"

"Because I am so much in love you with you, I prefer to die for you!"

"No, you must not say that, none of us is going to die. In fact, we have just started our lives!"

I laid beside her, she put her forehead on my forehead and said, "If I should have a baby today, I am going to name him or her after you." Instinct told me we should be heading home now before it starts to rain. We could not reach the market as promised, even though I did not want to go in the first place, but I used the rain as an excuse. "I really wanted to get some stuff!" she moaned.

"Why don't you go quickly and come back?" I suggested.

"You must not disappear like you did to me last time. I came back and you had gone, so we should leave here together," she responded, "or else."

***

Chapter Ten

Nowadays, I don't do too much. Two of us. It would be delightful to get a companion in the farmhouse. "In fact, I would love her to come with me," I said to myself silently, I was quite sure she would not overhear me.

***

The Chief Hunter is in a strong position of power. Whoever is in that position possesses significant power in the Yoruba land and people are usually afraid of them because of their wonderfully energetic, demonic and freaky power to conquer and always win a position. They have foresight, that is power to see beyond the end of the argument, to determine what would happen within the next hour or before any sudden happenings. He can predict that it is going to rain and so it would be. He may tell you don't go out there, because there is trouble or a riot outside and you better believe that is exactly what is happening.

He is usually tall and has a huge personality. He is charismatic. A Chief Hunter is fearful. Handsomeness is not one of their traits, but you often find women in love with them. They are physically fit, who can engage in physical combat with a lion or tiger. Their physique is unorthodox and incomparable; moreover, they often do a lot of running in the bush, running a long distance of miles without stopping. Some animals, like the cheetah, usually run and hide from them.

Some of their juju medicines are very strong because you may think you see him now, but in a few minutes when you check, he is really not there, especially if something evil is going to happen to him. Where he disappears to are unknown destinations; or you may happen to see a snake or any different kind of reptiles crawling, this is a sign, and it means that the Chief Hunter wants to show himself to you and to tell you that he recognised you and would deal with you later on.

Sometimes they lead the war if they choose to or stay behind, depending upon their choice. In fact, the King usually lets them choose where they would like to stand or be in the time of war. Sometimes they are very cocky; they would make the rejected people of their town, like thieves and prisoners, go to the war front. These were easy kills. Their ruthlessness meant that they usually don't have enemies in the town.

If there was no war, he would order the whole neighbourhood to go and fetch fire woods, palm leaves and fill a thief's house with them and light it on fire and burn it down with their belongings. If the wife or family attempted to escape, they would get shot by a gun. People would be dancing around the house that is on fire while singing a song.

The song goes like this:

A o poko dile ole poko, a o poko dile ole poko, e poko dile ole, poko. Ole ko dara lawujo, e poko dile ole poko, poko dile ole poko. Ole ko dara inile ife, e poko, ao poko dile ole poko, e poko dile ole poko. Awa ko fole inile ife, poko e poko dile ole poko.

Now you get the glimpse of the Chief Hunter's character and his influence. He does not take any nonsense from anybody except the King, who is the boss of all and whom people respect. This title of Chief Hunter is bestowed by the King; only the King can choose who the next Chief Hunter would be, he cannot be influenced or bribed when choosing the right person. There is only ever one Chief Hunter at a time.

***

Chief Hunter

However, I came back from bush to the town because of the rain. I was being lazy about going out because of the wetness. I felt like relaxing for the rest of the day. I said to my wife, "Why don't you go and do the cooking in good time and then join me?"

"All right, darling," she said and walked away, and a few minutes later I smelt one of my favourite dishes, but I could not smell it for long as I drifted in to sleep.

I was half awoken when I felt her bottom subtly touching my pelvis. She held my penis, the erection was stiff and hard. Then she dropped it, as if she felt a shock.

"Why?" I asked.

"I felt some kind of chill in my body; therefore, I could not hold you when you were so strong," she replied.

"OK, I give you permission to hold it."

"No, no permission," she was agitated and got hold of it and gently put it in her mouth. "Too fat," she replied, "and long, my mouth is always so full of it that I cannot get a breath out, else it is something I love to do all the time."

While it was in her mouth, I was feeling a kind of excitement that I myself cannot explain at all, but my two legs were moving as if I was swimming in the river and I was giggling. Suddenly, she stopped and put it in between her two legs. I could see some of the spasms in her mouth as she drew my head close to her mouth and kissed me. We clenched tight against each other.

I must show her what I am capable of, I thought to myself. I am not an easy man to deal with, occasionally she must know me. I must remind her. So, I disappeared from our bed in the town, to the farmhouse near the bush. I knew when she woke up she would be amazed and would be looking around for me.

I felt someone, in my state of disappearance, following my trail to the farmhouse. I could be very unpredictable in these circumstances, if it is an enemy I could easily kill. As I was trying to wear my clothes, she joined me. "How are you?" she said in her usual voice.

"You follow me, Tes!" I responded. She must also have disappeared. I didn't like it; I became jealous of her.

"Please, please don't, don't, I love you," she cried. I changed to unarmed insect and flew outside the hut. I heard her crying, then I walked back inside.

"I told you that you shouldn't disappear on me", she calmly said.

"Is that a warning?" I shouted.

"NO, No!" Tes said.

"You don't warn me, I am the husband who saw you and brought you home, your safety is in my hand."

She responded, "Your protection likewise is in my hand." Then she rushed to me and smacked my chest three times, and rested her head there. I calmed down. She said forgive me. The argument was over, we kissed and made up. I did not expect that Tes could disappear and follow me on my trail. *I don't like it.* I thought I was the only one who could do that!

I later found out that even the Little Hunter could do the same.

***

Chapter Eleven

Tes' Story

The Chief Hunter usually expressed about Tes that it was ideal for her to marry someone as powerful as him. She too possessed a supernatural power and was a strong lady; she also had freaky, demonic, powers. Yet, she had a pure heart, lovely, one you would like to cherish.

Tes, at first, was the only child of her parents. Before her birth, her parents dreamt of her as having all kinds of witchcraft power because the village where they came from was a witchcraft dominion. But there was one lady in that village who fought against the witchcraft because she believed in the power of a god to good.

This lady usually fought the evil power with leaves that she would go and fetch from the bush. The lady knew every leaf in the bush by their name and knew what they could be used for. It was her gift from heaven; you would tell her your problem and she would only ask you to come back the next evening to get what to use. She would go to the bush as soon as you left and fetch fresh leaves. At times, she would burn, boil, grind and crush them with some other things and show you exactly how it should be used. She would then ask you to come back and give your gratitude. Exactly like what the

Chief Priest would do, but the differences in their power meant some people preferred to use the Chief Priest than this lady.

The lady lived for almost 200 years before she died. She actually died with Tes's mother caring for her. It was a week later, on the same day, and at the same time she died that Yetes was born. The abbreviation of her name is 'Tes', which means the 'old woman come back'. Yetes was 5ft 5ins tall, very dark black, and she was very pretty. From birth she had been showing her magical power and freakishly disappearing from one place to another or making you disappear from the vicinity. She knew everything about the leaves in the bush. She started walking at the age of 5 months and talking at the age of 11 months. She told her parent to not look any further for another child because she was the only one they were going to have. (Except if her mum went to another man outside the marriage.)

Her parents were aristocrats but had only one difficult, powerful child. Yetes had always been very helpful, kind, quiet, calm and trustworthy. One time a lady went to fetch water from the river. At the riverside she was bitten by a snake called a black mamba. As she was shouting for help, Tes was also on her way to fetch water, the lady was so loud that her shouts drew a crowd to her. Tes said give her to me and she turned around and got some leaves. She squashed those leaves in her hand and what she said to it nobody knows, she drained the squashed leaf water onto the wounded leg where the snake had bitten. Within five to ten minutes, the lady seemed to be dozing away; Tes asked the brother of the lady to take her home, then Tes declared that after the lady had slept she would be all right. It was true, she woke up in the evening on that day and she was shown where to find Tes to thank her.

Tes' performance was quite fascinating. It won praise and fear amongst the villagers. The village where her family lived was always so tense. Children were hardly allowed to play outside. A sunny day or an evening when the mist set over the village were the most dangerous periods. Those were the times when the witches hunt children. But Tes could play at any time. On one occasion, Tes asked her mother, "Why am I the only one with nobody to play with? The boy I used to play with, I cannot find him anymore. Again I went to his house; the parents were crying. Can you tell me what happened? They will not tell me what happened."

"He is dead," her mother responded

"What do you mean by that?" she asked.

Her mother explained.

"Can you take me there please to see him?" asked Tes.

Tes' mother felt reluctant and said, "Tes, I don't want any problem."

"I am not a problem child, mother," she said.

"OK."

They both went to meet the parents of Jambi, Tes' friend, at home. When there Tes made a request to see the boy alone. "I would like to see where you laid down the boy's corpse," she demanded. The boy's parent insisted to Tes' mother, "No, we must not because we are afraid that she may go the same way as Jambi."

"I cannot," Tes said.

"She was here almost four times today, she saw us crying and she would not go back, that is why his father went to buy the coffin to bury him," Jambi's mother continued.

"Well, Tes wanted to see him," replied Tes' mother. So Jambi's mother opened the door and there was Jambi lying down face-up. Tes called his name, "Jambi, Jambi, Jambi! How many times have I called you to get up and follow me now?"

Jambi's mother said, "This is why I don't want her to come in here because of the distress it causes her."

Suddenly, after about three to five minutes, Jambi woke up and called Tes to thank her, "Thank you," the boy said.

"Your mother has been crying since yesterday, and your brother and cousins – every one of them – have been crying for you."

"I only had a good sleep, Tes," the boy said and they both went out to play.

Everyone was astonished that Tes woke him up. The father came back with the coffin only to find that his son was playing outside. He could not believe it; he threw down the coffin and ran inside. "What happened? What happened?," he repeatedly asked. The boy's mother said that Tes woke him up, and Jambi said that he was only having a long sleep. Everyone came to know Tes and her power, and now truly knew that the old lady was still around them; they were glad that the village would be safe, so people started dancing. Jambi's father went out to get drinks and some alcohol for everybody to celebrate that the son who died, had come back from the grave.

On the same day two other boys were saved by Tes. A great surprise was that as these boys woke up, you suddenly heard that an elderly lady somewhere had died. What killed her? The children that woke up sent her to the grave. This was witchcraft. Tes became well-known in the village. Her parents grew very cautious; they didn't want anything to happen to Tes, so Tes was sent to the town to live with a royal relative.

The village started to grow back again as more and more children were born. Tes' parents had a strong desire for another child, this was especially as Tes now lived in the town. They begged Tes and she instructed them to give a sacrifice. After this, they were able to conceive. So, they became a proud family of a girl and a boy. However, the day her mother got pregnant, Tes contacted her that she was going to have a boy and that she did not actually mean what she had said when she was younger and she was being childish. This was when Tes was about fifteen years old. Her mother responded by saying that Tes never ceased to amuse them.

Since Tes reached the town, she took it easy and concentrated on doing what she was told. Of course, she did, as she lived with the King. So she was well protected and focused on her education. On occasions Tes showed her wondrous power wherever there was trouble, and if she thought she could not defend herself, she would rather disappear.

***

Chief Hunter

I was still lamenting on Tes' disappearance trick.

Where did I get to know her before we got married? From the palace of our King, of course. The King is not weak, he is very strong because that position is of utmost importance, the first and the voice of the town. Even if you are not strong before you get to the throne, whenever you get that seat, you will definitely be as strong as a stone.

I thought to myself that I should probably give her more respect then. Moreover the wife of a strong man like me in the town must not be weak because many women and men would test her strength, especially a beautiful woman in her class. So, I succumbed and I asked her "What would you like me to do for you?"

She answered, "I've told you not to leave me on my own or disappear when you are with me."

"From today onwards do not emphasise my behaviour; all you need to do is accept me for what I am," I argued back.

"Don't tempt me! If not, you'll see my own powers. I know who you are and you know me. Why should we be fighting each other?" Tes retorted.

Instinct said to me she was as wise as a dove. I felt guilty and responded, "No, I am not tempting or doing this to get on your nerve. If it seems that I am fighting, could you please let us forgive and forget, because I would never apologise to anybody, you know that. But Tes, I love you." A tear dripped down her face, before it dropped I caught it and she lodged her head into my chest and I bent slowly and kissed her forehead and we were done with it.

She said, "You must be feeling hungry, now let me look around and see what we can cook from the farm."

"While you do that, I will go and check some of my traps."

***

Chapter Twelve

Chief Hunter

"Chief, you did not take one or two things which you always take with you from home, we are in the bush. So you will need your rod and your waistband with you," Tes said. So I went and took them and I said, "I didn't want to take them because I would not be far away from my hut in the bushes."

Generally, anytime I am going out into the bush for hunting at night, I have to dress up wearing a bante. I carry my rod and a forehead light attached to my headband. The headband has a special incantation that disables any animal which attempts to attack my head. They would not find it and they would become miserable not knowing what they are fighting.

I took my two kumos (rod), both short and long. I wore two ifunpa (armbands) on both hands, which have four eyes. Any animal that looked at my hands would be hypnotised, or turn back, then I would be able to shoot them or catch them. I wore one waistband. This was given to me by my mother, may her soul rest in peace. It is for protection, but I wear it like my jewellery, all the time on my waist. I sometimes wear about six to ten oundes, each of which do different jobs. Time has changed, sometimes all these oundes are too heavy and disturb you when running, so I swallowed some of the medicine put on oundes instead.

Although there are still one or two which I found difficult to swallow. This was due to my own laziness; some people still prefer for us to be wearing them because it shows how heavy and gorgeous you are with medicine and how powerful you are. Most especially when we are meeting at the palace with the King, you would see some people with their body covered in bloodstains because they just made a sacrifice to those protections and slept in the blood before coming to meet the King. This is to show the King they are always ready for any eventuality.

Someone like me can make one or two of your oundes disappear from your waist and that would make you look like a fool, an idiot who never got ready or prepared at all. I am also prepared to make all the oundes you are wearing disappear without you getting any protection at all, because when I cause them to disappear, you will lose all your power and would not remember anything at all. Occasionally, we often have a confrontation whereby everyone has to be proud and boast of what they have got, sometimes in front of the King and sometimes when we are fighting in the bush. We often kill each other for this or some people disappear and you never see them again, or get buried into the ground and never come back out again. I kept these thoughts to myself and dashed outside to check my animal traps.

We always found it easy to make traps because this was another way of hunting without sleeping out in the bush. This provided additional or substitute prey for what we caught Two of my traps had caught large rodents; *they were not dead yet, most probably they were caught this morning,* I thought. I took my kumo and whacked them on their heads and put them in my sacks and continued to check the rest of the traps. I had got ten of them to check. Sometimes there are twenty; it depends on how busy I am – I make ten whenever I am too tired. The third and the fourth did not catch anything, the fifth caught a python. The stupid idiotic snake must have come to eat my catch and got caught, I said to myself, so I did what we normally do whenever we cannot carry too much, I put the python down, put some big leaves on it to cover it and went to check the rest of the traps. I thought to myself, later I will come back and remove the leaves, and drag it to the farm house where I would tenderly remove the skin and dry it up.

While continuing with my checks, my sack had become too heavy. The next two traps I went to check caught bush pigs alive, not too small and too big for me to carry. So I headed towards the farm. Lucky enough, Tes came to meet me on the way, trying to find me, and helped me carry the two bush pigs. She saw the python and was afraid and could not touch it. Still she went to it and cleaned it up and roast the meat accordingly.

"Leave everything to me, I will look after them", she said, "while you go and take a shower," so I left her.

While I was in the shower, there was a snake trying to cross and get inside the farmhouse. I killed this one with my bare hands. "Look what I have got for you, Tes."

"Where did you find this?"

"I found it while I was trying to get access to the bath shed and so I killed it."

She looked at me in amazement, "And you killed it with your hands, are you sure?"

"Then with what would it be? I was about to have my shower and she was trying to pass through the left side of the shed to the bush, she must have smelt some food there."

Looking helpless, she stared at her bare hand and repeatedly said, "By your bare hands?"

"Yes. Tes. Why so surprised, was it because the snake was a small snake?" The type was called a rattle snake, big enough to swallow a rodent or bush cat. I left her to continue and I went to shower. Not long after I finished and I overheard her singing. She must have been too busy, that is when you see women singing to themselves to keep the job moving on without being disturbed. I dressed and came out to join her to look after the kills and sort them out for cooking.

"You are very quick," she said.

"There is a lot to do and it would be pathetic to leave you alone to do them."

"Thank you. Love you," she replied.

I dug a big hole in the ground. She had already cut the python into three feet pieces and we had six pieces on the ground. I made a fire and put them into it one by one till I cooked the whole lot of the python. *Good money*, I thought to myself. "Cook the second one and make a pepper soup of it," I told Tes. She responded that would be part of the dinner tonight.

She served vegetable soup made with snake liver, kidney mixture, its dick and heart. It was delicious because you could see the vegetable, which was so green and dark from the process of it cooking in the stew. I loved it and ate it with a keg of palm wine. I then brought out my tobacco pipe and smoked some. We started playing hide and seek till we both got tired and I caught her and started to tickle her. She was laughing and laughing until she started to tickle me. We were both engaged in child play outside until it started getting dark and we had to go indoors, yet we carried on playing until it was very late. I knew the time would definitely be going on to the twelfth hour. "I need to go and have my shower. Would you eat before I go, my dear?" I asked, "I have not seen you eat anything except little pieces of the vegetable, darling."

"That is enough for me."

"I would like you to eat. Because of our wishes you need to eat so that the worm inside you can get something to grip on so when God grants our prayer, there would not be any problem of insufficient this and that."

"I can understand what you mean. Would I lie to you, darling? I do eat, but anytime I am with you, I seem too full up. I don't get hungry in time," she replied.

"OK, before we go to bed, we do have to eat something together."

"OK," she said and went to make cassava *(eba)*. We both ate together until she was full, and I said to myself what she needs is love and my encouragement to eat, which means we should be eating together always. I could monitor how she ate and none of us would ever starve, I promised; except drinking and smoking, in which, I will never engage her.

***

Chapter Thirteen

Chief Hunter

Now I can see that the affection and love was just too much, she cannot do anything without me. *I have to keep her occupied, make her useful, let her do something significant and be content as an independent woman. That is how I want my woman to be.* I would like people to learn from my ideas, especially how I deal with my women, especially my wife. Let them ask me how do I cope with my woman? Give her liberty to talk and express her own opinion. Unlike our King, none of his wives can talk in his presence or express themselves or their opinion on a point. Not only our King, likewise all of the men from the dark ages are so rigid in character. I have been different to them all in attitude and affections. Of course, she knew it and I love her for real. I don't emphasise on it like she used to do most of the time.

I could not sleep; I was just looking at my surroundings and her. I loved the way she slept, her head was on my chest, the left hand was around my back which she used to stroke down to my waist. She slept on top of me, because sleeping this way showed the enormous interest and love between two partners. This is the way she used to sleep. I wondered how she coped whenever I was away for a week or two; she must have missed me so dearly.

I always check my surroundings before I sleep, at around the third and fourth hours of the morning. At that time, I either go out for or come back from hunting. So, I gently put her head down on the pillow and her hand which was across my back on the bed. Then I walked away from the bed with my light and checked our surroundings were safe and secured, then came back to bed to sleep. As I silently lay down, she said, "Where did you go to in the middle of the night without your kumo? Chief, never do that again. Can you promise me you will never do that again? Anytime you go out there, please, I beg of you, always take your kumo or your killer ounde with you."

I said, "You are too afraid of me getting into trouble."

"Yes, I don't want you to get hurt, injured or get bitten by a terrible snake that is looking for its own dinner."

Without much argument I supported what she said and promised her I would not do so again. "I don't know you will wake up with me, Tes."

"Any little thing can wake me up. In fact, I had already woken up when you put my hand from your back down to my side. I just said to myself where is he going again, I thought you were going to the toilet."

"No, I always look around the house and outside twice before I sleep back again."

"Everything you do always meets my approval and that is why I would always love you and thank you for the family being properly protected and there being no threats to our family safety and security." This was her distinction towards me.

This time around Tes could not wake up. It was around the eighth hour in the morning. I washed and went outside to do some planting and made sure that the yam plantation was healthy, as were the maize and the beans. There was a little bit of cultivation which I was planning to do a long time ago. I was doing that when Tes called for me to eat. This was around midday. I don't normally eat in the morning, like most people do, she knew that occasionally I may just request traditional tea. "Ding, ding, ding, ding!" she rang the bell that I should come inside to eat. When I looked up the sun was already high in the sky!

"I could not believe it," I said.

"You have been working and not looking back at all," she replied.

"You are absolutely correct. You see, Tes, that bell you rang, I normally don't use it. We always use it when there is problem. You will see, if there are any of the hunters around, they will surely be in touch to make sure everything is all right before they go back home."

Not so long after, as Tes was setting the table, and as I was asking what we will be eating, we heard, "Hellooooo…ooo E ku onile o, Ago onile o, Ago ya o."

"Ema wo ile o," said by Tes. She knelt down on her two knees, which showed the person was an adult, especially one of my friends or someone known or familiar to her. It was the Deputy Chief Hunter. As he came towards me, he quickly turned back and shook his bottom three times and gave me a warm handshake, bringing my hand to his forehead chest and mouth. That is how we hunters greet the elder, this is especially when they greet me. Those who knew me, respect that I am the only one, next to the God of Iron *(Ogun)*.

I took enough amount of what I would like to eat from the bowl of beans and corn, then offered the bowl to him and from him to her.

"My Chief," he said, "what type of meat is this?"

"Of course, you are eating bits and pieces of python, rodent and bush pig meats."

Having taken the amount of what I need, I passed the bowl of meats to her.

"Whoa, whoa, whoa, the smell is fantastic, delicious and pepper rich. My Chief, this is the secret to your looking younger and healthy."

"Thank you," I said.

"Tes is cooking good food for you."

"Thank you," I said again and took my tobacco and drew a smoke and passed it to him and left him and Tes on the table. I went away into the farm and continued with my work.

***

Chapter Fourteen

Chief Hunter's Wife, Tes

Any husband who could ever provide, that is a complete man, I thought to myself. It is not his first time or second time, I have been watching him checking our surroundings several times. He ensures my safety and security. I believe that is why he was made the Chief Hunter.

"My wife doesn't ever cook like this, why?" Deputy asked me.

"I don't know how she does her cooking. Depends on the ingredients she uses. Do you know the type of ingredients she uses?"

"No, I don't know. You are her friend; can you talk to her about this please?"

"Ha, ha, ha!" I laughed. "No, no, no, that is not possible, because she is an elder woman. Of course, we know each other, but it is disrespectful for me to tell her or engage her into a discussion of this nature. If she comes here, tastes my food and wishes to ask me how I cook so deliciously like this, then we would talk, woman to woman. She would also need to ask me how I do my cooking, then I would tell her and give her the ingredients and she could learn that type of cooking from me. Else, there is no way to advise an elder woman how to cook."

As we were discussing this, another hunter knocked the door. I did not know him.

"Hellooooo…ooo Ago onile o."

"Ago ya," the Deputy answered and I opened the door and let him in.

"How is my Chief Hunter?" he asked.

"He is all right."

"Well, I heard the bell and that is why I said, I should finish one or two things I'm doing before I come here. I hope nothing is wrong?"

"Certainly, nothing is wrong; there is no problem," I repeated. He hesitated. "I am telling you the truth; it was just a false alarm," I urged. Then the Deputy intervened, he now looked at his direction and expected a conducive answer. Like Chief Hunter told me before he went out, a few of them would come around because they would think something must be wrong. The Deputy said, "It was false alarm because Tes was moving an object which caused the bell to ring, and probably it had been a long time we had seen our friend, that is why the bell rang. Isn't it a long time ago that it rang?"

"You are absolutely correct; it was quite a long time ago," he replied. They both giggled, before the Deputy finished his conversation, I already brought out some kola nuts for him to chew on his way out.

"What a pleasant woman!" the hunter said and started to praise and pray for me. "You will get old with your husband and may your two eyes not see evil again, for your father bore you and buried your wrongs, your mother bore you and buried your wrongs. May the work of evil and sins depart from you as of this moment onwards. Amen. Thank you very much. Say hello to your husband when he comes back and tell him the man next door, who doesn't like his guts, he would know, came to investigate. Once more, thank you again for the kola nuts."

"Thank you, sir" I said and he departed.

"As I was saying," said the Deputy, trying to get me back into conversation where we left it, "I shall arrange when we can meet you at home."

"So, you love my cooking so much?"

"Very, very, much indeed. If I was yet to marry, I would have been taking away food from you all the time."

I laughed, "Hah, hah, hah! Thank you."

"Well, I am on my way out as well and many thanks for everything, indeed."

"My hunter, huh," I said, "don't say this, kola nuts are too small an amount for you," and I gave the Deputy Chief Hunter the remaining two kola nuts. He was happy and started to pray for me. "Your stomach will get pregnant and your back you will use to carry and rear the child, by the grace of Almighty God and our God of Hunter, amen. I thank you for the special food and the kola nuts. Tell our Chief I have gone and I would see him again." So, they all departed.

I need to go and see my darling; he must be very tired now, I reckoned. So, I took some kola nuts, dried meat, and his special brew to drink. One thing I forgot behind was his tobacco pipe. After all, I don't want him to smoke or he may already have got something to smoke in the farm.

***

Chapter Fifteen

Chief Hunter's Wife, Tes

I could hear him singing his usual, "Ero ilu Ojeje, Ojeje e ba mi ki baba mi oje je e ba mi ki mama mi oje je wipe isu to fi si ile o, o je orogun ma mu je oje je isu ewura to kon gogo oje je lorogun ma fun mi je Oje je." He sang the same song over and over again, while making the bed to plant yam. In fact, I could not believe the enormous job he had done – great performance and all alone. It was like two or three people working in the same place.

The yam plantation was like a field where children play football. I was delighted and got more affectionate with him because of what a hardworking person he was! The maize farm was also exactly like a field, plus he would look after the cocoa farm and the palm trees. I succumbed to these signs of affection and said, "Darling, darling!"

He dropped what he was doing and said, "Are you all right?"

"Yes," I said, "I miss you."

"I missed you too. I just wanted to put the finishing touches to this line I am making for the yam, then I'll call you."

"Well, I am here now", I said, then he lifted me high up to the sky and brought me down to his chest and give me a golden kiss. I loved it because such a kiss would take as long as you two could endure. "By tomorrow we would be going to the town," said Chief.

"Are you fed up of this place?" I asked.

"No, no!" said the Chief.

"Then why? I am getting to love the life here," I replied.

"When I stay here I work and work nonstop, that is why I don't like to stay too long," said Chief, "so as soon as I finish, I just come home because I am longing to see you. When I come home, I rest and rest."

"I can see it," said Tes. "Thank you, my love." Then, I brought out what I had for him in my handbag

"Ho, ho, ho delicious!" he said as he saw the kola nut, then he questioned me, "Who asked you to bring this for me?"

"I reckoned it is all right and there is nothing as good as a kola nut after a hard day's work," I said instantly, "and that is why I brought it for you." As he took it from me, he opened it and they were in five pieces. He put one in his mouth and while attempting to put one inside my mouth, he said, "hah, hah" to me. As I was about to say ha, my mouth opened and he put it inside for me to chew.

Basically, kola nuts are sour but when you are swallowing its juice, that is when you feel its sweetness. It was my first time of chewing kola nut, but I did not let him know that.

"Don't you like it?" he asked.

"Yes of course, I liked it," I said, he put the second one in his mouth and chewed and asked if I wanted another one. I said yes, I took it from him this time so that he did not to put it in my mouth, and I kept it in my pocket handbag for later use.

He sat down, and I asked, "You need your pipe?"

"Yes, my darling."

"I could not bring it," I said.

"Of course, I've got one I made inside here." He went into his baste's pocket (which was sewn around his waist with the flap to cover the genitals) and brought out a rolled tobacco like a Havana cigar. He then took out two stones and scratched them together and lit his half-smoked hand-rolled tobacco. He blew the smoke into my face, I felt I would not like it and should tell him off; he had never done that before. But I quite liked it, it smelt nice and not strong that I could not withstand; in fact, I liked it and I always put my nose up trying to sniff the smell of his tobacco. I believe he put something into it, what it is I don't know. I left that for future enquiries. Maybe this could be something I could use to make decent money out of, another trading outlet. If I put everything in front of him now, he may not like to tell me but some other time, you know when he is feeling tender and ready for love. He would do anything and give anything to satisfy me.

"Tes, could you please check where we put our water tank *(Amu)*? You will find my keg of palm wine, please bring it out for me, it must be cool and cold to drink now."

"Yes darling, but I've got your special brew *(burukutu)* here for you."

"I love you; how do you know you are supposed to bring it for me?"

"I just saw it is a day with the sun shining. After a pleasant day of hard work, you need to relax with your *burukutu*; that would make your day."

"Bless you," he said, and I gave him a piece of meat I had brought. "Look, I want you here always. Everywhere I go, everywhere I went, everything I do is for you, Tes." I was exceedingly happy and he grabbed my head with both hands and kissed me gently.

"Shall we be heading towards home now in the town or sleep here till very early in the morning and then go to the town?" he asked me.

"I haven't packed all our stuff, especially the drying meats for selling. I think we should wait till tomorrow afternoon because we have much to take with us home."

"I didn't realise that we got plenty already. So should I still go for kill tonight?"

"May I suggest no."

"Why?"

"We must think how we will carry them home. Already we had enough."

"All right, all right, let's wait and play," and he started to tickle me under my arm as I lifted my hand to drive away the fly on my forehead and then ran outside the farmhouse. I went after him because I wanted to tickle him back, but I could not catch up with him, as he was running to the river adjacent to our farmhouse.

He suddenly jumped into the river. *I was confused and ask myself why did he jump in the river?* He tickled me, ran away, and jumped into the river, I could not add them together, but I later realised that he did not want to take a shower so he preferred to swim in the pool of water instead. So I followed. Before I jumped, he had been saying, "Come on in, come in, Tes."

I joined him.

"So you can swim?" Chief asked.

"Not much," I said, he took a dive and went under the water. I did the same and I found him and we both lifted our heads out of water together which was very exciting. Then I said, "I must not lie, this was my first time of swimming in the river. Of course, I was not afraid since I'd had people discuss about swimming and asked them what to do and not to do should I happen to be in the river. Not knowing I would be taken swimming by my husband!"

In my dreams of a perfect husband when I was single, I hoped for a man who would make me laugh and loved me, but I never knew that there was more to it than just love and laughs. What about excitement, inspiration, security and adventure? My Chief has it all. If I did not come with him into the farm, I would just remain and love him, that would have been it all. But joining him and seeing his true picture made me more loving and helped me understand that he was the type of man I wanted and exactly what I prayed to get in life. What am I to him? I don't know, I know he loves me and shows the type of security he has for me and has promised to satisfy me in life. What else do I need? Nothing more. I remained bubbly.

From the river he carried me on his back to the farmhouse. On our way, we passed one person. I did not care to acknowledge that he would talk about seeing me on Chief Hunter's back. Then Chief told me, "Look, this is going to be talk of the town that I carried my wife instead of me carrying a child. Some people would even say I carried goat on my back. I would not be surprised if the King summons me to the palace."

Chapter Sixteen

Chief Hunter

As I put her down on our bed, she seemed to wake up; she didn't know she had been feeling sleepy on my back. "Are you sleeping?" I asked.

"No," she said.

"But you sound sleepy, dear. You are so lovely, why not sleep?"

"I'm great, thanks," Tes responded.

Then she abruptly woke up and said, "I will cream your body with my own type of oil which was made with coconut and is full of moisturisers, which will make your body smooth and get rid of the dryness and scaliness. This is a major reason I don't want you to touch my body, sometimes the simple reason is because of the way I feel when you're inside me."

"Don't you know how I feel when your hand touches my naked body?" I replied.

She held on to my penis, which stood so erect and strong that we could not resist it. I said to let me inside now. She stood up and opened her legs and let me into the main entrance of her vagina; without too much pushing, it went straight inside. But she always buried her head on my chest, sometimes looking for my mouth for a kiss. I always think she makes me to do most of the hard work while she is just relaxing on my chest. We continued until we both fell asleep.

I have been used to waking up at the fourth hour of the morning. Over the night, she had already packed all our things and was ready to go to the town. I slightly held her foot and touched the heel of her feet, then she woke up.

"Are you all right?" she asked.

"Yes, you have to wake up now, and we must be on our way home."

"Ho no, not today but tomorrow," she said.

"Tes, Tes, you have to wake up now, darling; this is the time we have to be on our way home."

"OK, kiss me," she asked, so I lowered my head down and kissed her. "Say Tes, I love you. Tes I, I, I need you," she requested again.

"No, no, not need. OK then, Tes I, I love you 100 times."

"No, say 1,000 times!" she said back to me.

"I will say 1 million times!"

She got up and wanted to take a bath.

"No Tes, you cannot bathe now. After all, we are just going home, you can easily bathe at home."

"Yes, you are right," she responded and got up to wash her face, which did not take very long and then we set up to go. Tes was now sitting down in the front of the bicycle carriage, while I was pedalling the wheels. Not too long after we left, our path in front was dark and you could hardly see anything at all.

I stopped and I said to her, "Do you know what is in front of you? That is an elephant. A group of them are eating and preparing themselves to go ahead in their journey."

"Can you please move forward so I can see them, and why is the whole place so dark?"

"It is the male elephant in front of us and perhaps with its female."

"Are they meeting?"

"Not really, they may be crossing or waiting to sleep overnight."

"Do they sleep?"

"Of course, yes."

"Are they sleeping while standing and not lying down?"

"Yes, that is how elephant and giraffe sleep. All animals sleep; I mean all creatures sleep, although the timing may be different to each other. These may take us a long time before we get home."

Should we wait, or should we go back to the hut?" she asked.

"We should wait."

"Can't we walk around them?" Tes asked.

"You dare not walk close to an elephant when they are eating or taking a break or sleeping. They are giant in size, likewise they are very fast and dangerous, they kill instantly and are ferocious in attitude, especially when one is disturbing their peace. They would not rush to attack you, but only one of them, their leader, is the one to attack whatever wants to endanger its family." After saying this, I went to the bush. I took some of the leaves and rubbed them in my palms and used it to wash my face and wash her face. Suddenly, Tes found that we both were on the other side of the elephant; what I did made her a little bit of drowsy.

"You are magical!" she said.

"Not magical, but we need to get home."

However, before we got home, I had to kill one antelope; two of them were very close on our way. I made her kill the other antelope by shooting the gun.

"He's dead, he's dead, Chief! I made a kill!"

"Of course, you are my wife. Everyone would be expecting you to know how to shoot a gun. This is the beginning and would not be your end, amen," I said. We put the antelopes on our carriage and were on our way. It was not too long before we reached home. I was desperately in need of sleep and I did not mess about with it, I just went to my bed and slept, leaving Tes to do the rest.

Unknown to me, she went to call her sister for help and they had both been working very hard. Until she came to spy if I was awake or not. Apparently, I was starting to wake up when I became very hard under there, I was thinking about Tes, and then she came in to our room.

"I just want to check to see if you are all right; how do you feel?"

"Very strong down here," I said.

"I am not asking you for that." As I put her hand down there, she knew there was nothing except to surrender to nature's call.

"You may likely get lot of visitors today," said Si.

"Why do you think so?" Tes responded.

"Because people kept asking for you both when you were away. Some people even remarked that you both don't go

89

away at the same time, but it is good to get the wife used to the farm. That says it all. They have missed your husband around, but, due to the nature of his work and the title, they believe his wife must be around to attend to the house."

"They better get used to it because he did not marry me for them, he married me for himself. This is our peak and I would need to get used to my husband."

"Whoa, whoa, whoa!" Si exclaimed, "What is going on? Anything different you will like to share with me about him?"

"Hey, this is personal. What do you, a little girl, want to concern yourself with? Do you want me to be discussing my affairs with you, little girl?"

Si had forgotten that Tes was not the type you could just interact with or a person who liked gossiping. She was loyal to her husband, so none could get in between them both. She hardly had friends. The King's youngest wife was Tes' friend. The last time we went to a party, they interacted a lot. Since then I thought Tes would like gossip. She didn't. So I stayed quiet because she deserved my respect.

I cleaned up and got ready to go to the palace and see the King. It's been a long time since I saw him; I need to take some of the killing to him, I told Tes and she started on the killings.

The next person to come to my house was the Little Hunter. He felt so excited, maybe because of Tes' sister, whom he has his eyes on. He could not say much to Si, just a polite interchange; with Tes they went on and on, until he broke it off and said, "Where is my Chief?" Seeing me about 200 yards away, he shook his bottom three times and turned around and we shook our hands up and down, up and down, up and down, then clenched on to each other's fingers, pulled outwards, and he kissed my hand.

"Where are you going?" Little asked abruptly. Before I answered him, he was even putting words in my mouth. "Are you going back to the farm?"

"No, I am going to see the King; it has been a long time since I have been in this palace."

"Come on then, let us go," he said, carrying the bag. We made our journey to the palace. We were met with the King's absence and had to leave everything for the first wife.

***

Chapter Seventeen

Chief Hunter

The first wife knew how to joke with me, not to the extreme, and I would not go beyond my boundary when talking to her. I cut it short and we were on our way home.

Little Hunter said, "My Chief, it has been a long time, and how are we preparing for this year's anniversary for Ogun?"

"Nothing much, we are going to do it as normal," I replied. "Moreover, the King is not in, that really causes me great concern. Whenever you see the first wife behave like that, it's a matter of concern, because of the few things she would not like disclose to me. But sooner or later I will know what is happening in the palace. I know for sure something is wrong."

"Should I be going home from here?" Little asked.

"If you would like to go, it is OK, and I shall surely be in contact with you, especially on this topic."

"My Chief," he replied, "the only jungle chief, the strong and the strongest one who can defeat the lion in its inhabitant" after saying this, Little proceeded ahead and went away.

I am not generally a happy man, many thoughts come to my head and such could have made my brain damage, as I was beginning to hate myself. Without knowing, I had reached home and ignored everyone outside the house, both people who were standing and sitting, including Tes, with all their welcome greetings. I ignored it all. I went straight to my bed in the power room. This room was personally for me and nobody was allowed to come inside, except with my permission. Well, I would not tell others not to enter, but you enter here at your risk, and I am the only remedy.

Tes was upset. I don't even care. I could overhear her mutterings and murmurings, "Why did you have to go inside there to sleep? Do you want to die on me? Do you want to kill me? Have I been unfaithful to you? Why do you have to treat me like this?" She started crying.

Instantly, I said, "Come in! "Come in here!"

"NO, NO! You come outside here," she said, "What have I done to you?" she asked.

I said, "No more," and I turned myself into a splash of water, of not more than a full cup, on the floor. She could see the splash of water moving towards her. She went to take a broom to sweep it away. Before she came back, I was on our bed in our room. As she went back to drop the broom, she inevitably saw me on our bed. She started to praise me "Ekun, Ekun", which means tiger, tiger, then she continued, "The only one of the jungle, who else can eat meat like you, because you will kill and kill and eat little. You kill ferociously, tiger, tiger." I had just changed back so I was very sweaty, so she got a little fan out to fan me until I sweated no more. She now lodged her head inside my armpit; as she was about to start questioning me, I said, "Stop."

"You know I love you; why did you ignore me in the presence of everybody?"

"I love you too, Tes, sometimes things happen, and expressions are so difficult to find in this case. You will need to just let me rest for a while and I will come back to you."

"No," said Tes.

"I am all right now, can't you see?"

"Yes, if you have to die, we should die together and that is why I am here with you. Get used to me and follow my eyes and body language which I use." She was so pathetic and loving; she always wants love. And that, of course, was her nefarious intention; she took in everything and learned more to help her in the future.

"One thing you must always remember is that you are no more alone, you are mine and I am yours to use as your tools. I've given my life onto you. If the result from the palace was not good enough, then you are supposed to call me and we could discuss about it together, you cannot go to your power room. I knew the King was your friend, don't let him take you with him, I still need you around me," she remarked.

I asked, "Do you think he wanted to take me with him?"

"Yes, yes, these powerful people, whenever they are dying, they usually take their friend with them, else they do not go. You will soon hear the King was all right and he is asking for his favourites, you and some other people that he loves."

"Well, he always asks for me when his all right."

"Of course, yes, you knew very well he is my cousin, and I know much of what was going on in the palace. However, I am here, you go nowhere until God says yes, for both of us."

What she said made me sceptical and wary about how I felt for the King. Actually, my state of mind had not been pleasant since I left the palace. I said to myself; *therefore, she must be correct in whatever she said.*

With immediate effect, I felt OK, there was nothing wrong, no more brain damage and I was as strong as ever. She took me in her arms and we both went outside. "Ekun, Ekun," everyone was saying and prostrating. I then said, "The God of Hunter bless all of you and give all of you happiness and joy for life." I asked them to get up and make merry with whatever they have in front of them. Tes had given the men some kola nuts and whenever my people see kola nuts, they pray, talk and talk, and discuss even important issues over the presence of kola nut. You can say kola nut is very much full of entertainment.

***

Chapter Eighteen

Chief Hunter

The women were pounding yam, and two women were assisting by putting the yam from the fire pot unto the pounding portal. The rest were talking and deliberating, with Tes watching and overseeing that the pounded yam was all right and would be delicious to eat. She left me with my friends.

"My Chief, how about the palace?" they asked.

"The palace was all right. But certainly, the King, as you know, was not around."

"Very sorry, very sorry," they were saying until the women started to serve the food around the table.

One of the men said, "The smell of the cooking would not let me go, until I eat out of it. It smells so delicious that it made me sit down and thank God our Chief is a happy man who welcomes everybody. No matter where you come from, or where you are born, you can join him on the table when he is eating, fill up yourselves and go on your own way."

So every one of them was asking me, "What about our festival? What about our anniversary?"

"Whoa, whoa, whoa!" I said, "Can you please be civilised and talk one by one?" Silence came upon them, and I asked the man in the middle. Tall and slim, he wore a red cap, his teeth were as dark as charcoal and he made it look as if there was no chewing stick to wash his mouth out.

He asked, "Is Ogun festival going to be cancelled?"

"No, the festival will take place on same day and time. You will all hear from me the fate of the palace. In fact, I would say to you today that there is no problem at the moment regarding the palace. Everything is all right, our King is all right, he is only travelling and most likely to come back on our festival day or so. There is no change of plan whatsoever."

With this little hint they were as fabulous as ever; they all ate and after this deliberation, they were leaving one by one until I saw the Little Hunter coming. He said to me, "I could not stay at home by myself with what happened and the way you felt when talking to me."

"Thank you, my Little Hunter, but the food has just been finished along with the drink."

"Don't mention that," said Tes, "Little, follow me."

Little followed Tes; Tes, no matter whether I am here or not, she will make you feel at home.

Conversations could be heard from every part of the house. I myself didn't knew when people invaded it, both men and women; of course, some of them I knew but most I do not know. Some of them I thought were here for Tes and came with their husbands and they were Tes's friends, but because of the number of people that sat down, Tes found it difficult to introduce them to me. This did not upset me, and I took it amicably.

What I observed vividly was most of the people wanted to know me and my wife and how the festival would be. I refused to make them think that the festival would be a failure.

I deliberately raised their hopes, and everyone was grateful and eager to spend, buying drinks and kola nuts from my wife.

It was later that I heard a few people had been deliberately sent to come and ask if this festival would take place. Rumours had spread beyond the palace on whether the unexpected would happen, if so there would not be a festival. The news from the palace may have triggered sadness. But, who is sending people to investigate?

When I looked around and tried to know who and who were around me, I found that most of my important men were not but they had sent people to visit me.

I knew people who were absent, my Deputy and the second in command, likewise some important people, although they were not ranked but everyone knew they were real hunters. My Deputy was someone of my height; in fact, you would mistakenly take him for me, not knowing he wasn't the Chief.

***

Chapter Nineteen

"My Deputy"

Deputy Chief Hunter is an important position and the person must be strong among the members. All the hunters gathered together and selected who would be Deputy and the Chief Hunter must not vote, he had to administer and to see that the selection went true and fair. On the day of electing the Deputy, the palace had to be aware, so, he would need to go to the palace for accession and reception. When going to the palace, they had to bring with them the favourites of the King, such as lion skins dried and worth sleeping on, raw yam, and between ten and twenty kola nuts.

Whoever brought all these items would definitely seek the attention of not only the King but the palace as a whole; even for any promissory title in the palace, one day you would be called to come and take a seat with the King. To show the King that you really worth it, you might as well go with the legs of the lion whose skins you brought. In fact, the majority of those who kill lions often do this as a present to the King. Not only to say they want the title but to prove to the King that they are strong men. Because when you sat down, the King would interrogate you about the killing, and how you performed to kill the predator.

So, the ordained would kneel down, the Chief Hunter would sit beside the King at the right and the King's Deputy sat at the left. No other chieftain would be there; if they were, they would need to sit down among the commoners. The King would put his irukere (the horse tail) or his sword on the Deputy's head three times, then on his left and right shoulders three times. After, he would ask you to proceed with happiness. Then we would all come back to the Chief Hunter's hall and celebrate till dawn. This procession is similar to when taking up a title of chieftaincy in the palace.

The Deputy Chief Hunter can also lead the war. He is always the person to lead the war and deputise for the Chief Hunter when he is not around. The liberty is that he can take over the Chief Hunter's properties, including his wife, if the Chief Hunter dies. Can the Chief Hunter inherit those of his Deputy? No. He cannot, but it depends on their relationship.

The second in command was just an ordinary title which is given to support the Deputy. There was no big ceremony as such. You just needed to dress nice as a hunter and if you are married, you must come with your wife and children to meet the Chief Hunter, the Deputy and their wives and children as well.

The Chief Hunter discusses with his Deputy and selects whom they think deserves to be their second in command. It's awarded due to one of their members' performances, articulation and loyalty to the hunting members and their subordinates. You don't need to provide skins, yam, or animals to eat, but all you need to do is cooking and distributing drinks within the members – provide food, drinks, kola nuts and bitter kola nuts. Everyone would be told and because of your generosity members will support you.

If you have the funds, we could celebrate till darkest hour of the morning. or dawn. You do not need to be strong in medicine or freakishly strong. You will be protected by the Chief Hunter and the Deputy in the war front or in case there was problem in the town or at home.

The support Chief Hunter provides for people in the town is remarkable, and this made both posts very important in the community and in the palace.

***

Chief Hunter

I wondered what Tes would be thinking right now. Could she be on the same thought as me? People have been departing gradually and gradually, we now have more and more spaces to manoeuvre and I have been getting more affectionate with my wife, whom I've been longing to see. She came so close and bent down for a kiss on my cheek and then mouth.

"Your mouth was sweetened," she said.

"It's the drink with kola nuts which I have been chewing that made my mouth sweet," I said. "How are you, since morning and I only briefly saw you this afternoon?"

"Ho yes, I am OK, darling."

"Why so many people today?" I asked.

"I thought as much that you will be asking yourself why these many people? It's your Deputy that kept sending people to find out about Ogun festival, and to come and see you to arrange to become member of hunters in our village."

"That was all right, they are masculine and muscled. However, none of them told me anything but instinct told me they were up to something. I hoped they have not misbehaved!"

"I was told they weren't. They were quiet boys raised up from the village and have got hunting in their blood or in their hands."

***

Chapter Twenty

Chief Hunter

"Has the date been fixed then?" Tes asked.

"I do not need to fix date, the date is when we see the moon on the sky, the second day after that is our festival, this is still a few months away."

"Much better, my Chief," Tes said.

"Tes, I could hear some people discussing or whispering out there."

"Ho yes, it's the Little Hunter and my cousin's sister"
They must have heard me, so they both came inside, while the Little Hunter saluted me as usual, "The Chief, the hunter of tiger and lion, who would dare look a tiger in the eyes. You are the one, the appearing and disappearing phantom, the man of quiet nature and always ready to fight at any time."

"Thank you, my little man," I said and showed him his seat.

I could sense there was something going on between the two of them; I looked at Tes and she was looking at me at the same time. Our four eyes met each other and Tes got up and came straight to me. I knew her plan, she thought her cousin would do the same thing towards Little Hunter. She must not because Tes was a very strict lady; she might give her a dirty smack on her face. I told Tes to get me some kola nuts, to bring my long pipe and give it to Little Hunter. She gave the pipe to Little Hunter, gave me the kola nut, and went back to her seat, very close to where her cousin was seated. The Little Hunter was very happy, he held the pipe and put fire into it from the fire made by the women during their cooking.

He inhaled from the pipe. One. Two. Three. Then puffed the smoke out gently through the air, and the blue smoke went straight to Tes's cousin. She turned left and focused on Tes. "Don't you like it?" asked Tes.

"I don't know, she replied.

The Little Hunter moved away from her sight and came close to where I was rested, which made us both more responsive to the conversation than we were before. He did not like that he would not be able to focus on Si, they were both trying to find love with each other. Finding love takes a lot of effort, some people do it through focusing, occasionally watching and gazing, conversations, and at the first sight. I called Tes's cousin to get me some cold water to drink. Little Hunter appeared to have been unsettled, as if he was actually the person who was sent the message.

He scrupulously adjusted himself while sitting down. "Are you all right?" I asked. "You looked as if you are not with me but about a thousand miles away." He burst out laughing and singing my praises, incantations of the Chief Hunter, "The man of major quietness, and a fierce fighter, knowing not how the end of a fight would be". I just smiled at him because he knew me very well. I gave him a kola nut to chew and passed the pipe with it. He drew a couple of puffs and held the pipe in his hand. He asked me, "My Chief?"

"Yes?" I said,

"Our festival is next month's end."

"No," I said. "The date is still far."

"What is the preparation so far? Is it going to be in the palace or here?" Two questions asked.

"My little man, the festival would be done the same way we have been doing things and there is nothing ambiguous in it. "We start from here, possibly go to the palace or remain here throughout, depending on information we get from the palace." Yet I could see that he really wanted the attention of my wife's cousin so simply I asked him, "Are you interested in my wife's cousin?"

"Ha, ha, ha," he pretended, laughing, "my Chief," he said, "you are a wise man with great understanding of human psyches." So, we both forgot the issue and Little Hunter was quite ready to go home.

The Little Hunter seemed to go away without much affection from my wife's cousin. Well, that does not matter, I reckoned and shrugged with my shoulder. This means that the Little Hunter needs to be aware that to get a woman to love you or get a woman to be married to you is not easy, as they used to say an uneasy head is not who wears the crown. While I said that to myself, I overheard Tes saying, "You didn't even say goodbye to the Little Hunter."

"It doesn't matter," she replied, as they both laughed it off and came inside the house.

"What are you having for the dinner?" Tes asked.

"Bit of yam and vegetable, and some fish would be all right." They went to the kitchen together and then Tes came with the plate of the food and her cousin came with water to drink and water in the bowl to wash my hands. "Thank you, my darlings," I said. They both stood around me and we were eating in the same plate together. This is the second time Tes's cousin would eat in the same plate with me.

Generally, eating in the same plate means a lot to people of our tribes, it means all of you eating together must not betray each other, and you must of course love each other, no matter what is happening. Especially, with someone like me, Chief Hunter, a man of iron and as strong as stone. So the hands we put in the plate means seeing each other's back and front hand. It is a symbol of affection for each other, which must be sweet as a honeycomb.

But with whom does she have the affection for? Is the affection of her cousin for me or for Tes? Else why should she dip her hand inside the same plate with me? Who would dare take light to look tiger in the eyes? Especially in the dark night, definitely nobody. She has touched my temper, I must show her what it means; if she has not been taught correctly in their home, she needs education from outside. Or her cousin, Tes, is supposed to make her understand how she should behave with me. *She should know she must not put her hand in the same plate with me!*

I kept it to myself. Tes did not know how upset I was, neither would I bring it to her knowledge. It seems Si looked into my eyes and I gave her the expression that I was not happy with her. Suddenly, I knew she herself had urges for me and that she deliberately did what she did, but my wife Tes did not have understanding of what she did, or could not recognise that she was not worthy to eat with me in the same plate. She, Si is too insignificant to be in the same class with me. It's disrespectful.

***

Chapter Twenty-One

Chief Hunter

Tes already had a bit of the palm wine; anytime, she drank she would be rushed to bed. In this case as she called me, I knew she was drunk and would like to sleep. I held her and supported her till she reached the bed safely and then I found one piece of cloth to cover her. She tried to make me sleep at the same time, but I refused and took her hand off my neck and straightened myself up. I went outside, a minute later she called her cousin to sleep in the living room where we all have the dinner. "OK, Tes," she said and came back outside to meet me where I was having my pipe and drink alone.

"I have wanted to do this for so long but don't know how to approach you," she said. Then she bent down and put her mouth into mine. I could not tell her off as I had intended to, only God knew what she put in her mouth that made her mouth so sweet. So I have to get on with it, she doesn't understand how effective it is whenever you meet somebody like me. First of all, I drew my hand into her little skirt and touching her vagina, then stroked up to find her breasts, and touching those I could certainly feel my blood running and her tits became so strong and the nipples were pointed as sharp nails. I gently held her hand on top of my erected penis and she could not hold it for long, and I gently pulled her down and slowly laid her on the ground properly. Then I suddenly realised she was still virgin who actually was in love with me. This made me remember that Tes, once upon a time, said there are no women in this village that I could not talk into being a girlfriend; they would say yes, they will always answer me and that both children and adults loved me so much, they would do anything at their power to please me.

I tried to penetrate into her, it was not easy. I held her close to my chest and her mouth seriously inside my mouth. My erection became so strong and I held the two nipples as I tried harder to penetrate my penis. It went *pow*, her vagina opened, and I made a deep penetration that made her hold on to me tightly, closer to her body. I almost bit off her nipple and began to ejaculate. Looking into her face, she was crying as well as happy. She was saying, "You must do it, I don't want to remain virgin anymore, I want to be proud that a strong man took my virginity away." I threw her off me. She got up abruptly begging, "Please, please, I would do anything you want," she said. Before my agreement, she was already on top of it, enjoying the deep penetration.

When I was about to take it out, she said, "No, no, please do not take it out. I am full of comfort and enthusiasm, after a sudden pain." I grabbed hold of my pipe and put a light unto it. She was on top of me, my erection was so stiff and strong and I could hold it as long as she liked. Moreover, she was the one to ejaculate. I pulled some strong smokes out while she continued to ejaculate until she said, "I am now tired, please can you release it?" It was just as if she knew that I wanted to cum but I was freezing and resisting not to. As she mentioned it, I released it inside her. She was so happy and promised not to tell anybody about our affections. I still wouldn't let her go free like that, so I grabbed the two breasts and squeezed them hard and twisted the nipples. This I was doing until she seemed to be falling asleep in my hands and I said, "Get yourself ready to go to bed, you are falling asleep," and I let her go to bed. Quickly, I looked around and cleaned the floor where there were bloodstains. She came back out and tried to clean; she cleaned everywhere and you could hardly suspect that something big was wrong, and as soon as she finished, she went straight to her bed and slept.

I said to myself there were no more little girls anywhere; everyone knows what they are doing. My thoughts were to tell Tes off about her behaviour, but knowing not she was attracted to me, and I indeed enjoyed it. Between her and Tes, which one do I enjoy most? This was a big question I was asking myself, and I could not figure out any answer to it, but one thing I knew, I loved my wife most and dearly, therefore there was no comparison. Sobbing in alcohol and tobacco, on the chair where I sat, I fell asleep. It wasn't too long I slept that I heard a tap on my foot's heel. I woke up, it was Tes who had come to wake me up to come to bed. Luckily, she didn't know or see us cleaning, she would have suspected and banned her coming here.

***

109

Chapter Twenty-Two

Chief Hunter

"One of these days, we are going to set the date, time and place for the festival. Tes, we must try our utmost to see it through. You know, the two of us are celebrants, may God please not let us be ashamed." I always said this prayer whenever I got something important or a major problem in my life, God usually helped me through my up and downs.

"Having said so, I really do not think it would be worth a while doing the festival this year. Why? My major objective has not been accomplished. Whenever I think about what people said to me, I do not want to do any festival at all." Tes looked around and said, "Is it because I have not been able to get pregnant for you?"

"Pregnant was one, having a child playing around was second."

She looked around and started to cry.

"Why do you always cry? Whenever I mention a child, you cry, I cannot express my opinion about a child anymore?"

"I suppose, sorry, sorry, Chief. It is my shame."

"No, no, do not say that," I said in a loud voice. "Listen Tes, it wasn't your fault, and nobody made it your fault, God provides those things. There is no way to enforce it. I know you will do it for me if it's your own making." We both counselled each other as well as triggered more annoyances. Throughout that day we were at each other's throats. Very impractical. It wasn't professional, unlike me. Anytime I happened to look in her face, her face was swelling, the two eyes were red, you would know she was not settled or happy at all. I wondered, *should I disappear and go away from her? No, that was not the answer or solution to this problem.* Then I needed to find solution to this problem, so she could remain at peace with me, because I still loved her.

Purely unprofessional of me, knowing not that her cousin was still around, noticing all the aggravation and mess that we were causing each other. Although, no words were uttered by her, she just kept her silence. We had our lunch and midday meal and were about to have the dinner when they both started talking with each other. I felt surprised and didn't like it at all but they were both mine. Let them shout for joy, then peace should reign!

Sooner or later I knew she would come back to me, she had no other acquaintances except me, and I knew she could not rest without me around her. She has been spying, sniffing and agitating to be on my shoulder again. She, without any gainsay, came and took my hand off my leg, where I was sitting down relaxing. She sat down and placed my hand on her pelvis and started to kiss my mouth, right cheek, left cheek and mouth, until I held her hair from behind and our four eyes became one. I gently put my mouth into hers and silently we both kissed and I took her to bed. On the bed we were, until her cousin said the dinner is ready and we should come and eat.

Of course I am getting much familiar with Si, Tes's cousin, no more insinuation and problems like before. I now made conversations and pulled her in. She drew a smile at my conversation without any problem. I thought Tes would have noticed, probably because of the argument in the morning, she could not be suspicious of my attention on Si, and I knew Si enjoyed my conversations a lot.

Yet I have to stop it, because I do not want her to get in trouble with Tes, or for Tes to forbid her not to come again. The more I tried to retreat, the more it seemed both of them were getting me into serious conversations. *Did Tes prefer me to be much closer with Si? Why? I was inclined to think, does she want me to be close with her? Or does she want me to make love to her, anything I said she always got her cousin into it,* "Perhaps, Si, how would you react to what Chief just said?" Tes would ask. Getting Si to talk with me became so much that Si herself looked into my eyes, suddenly wondering what was causing this. In the past, Tes would say it was between her and her husband, and if Si jumped into our conversations, Tes would smack her face or mouth.

However, my instinct said to me, *maybe she thinks I fancied her or what? Did she know I made love to her? Or she wanted me to make love to her and see if she could get pregnant?* My wife was very tricky and I knew that for sure. I knew her aim was to push her to me. But I could not because of the Little Hunter, who had been trying to seek Si's affection and love. He was desperately in need of a woman, but in this situation, what would the Little Hunter do? *If he knew what was going on in my yard, would he stop bothering over Si?* Anytime I try to converse about Little Hunter, she shrugs it off anyway, as if she did not like him.

Moreover, how would I be able to express myself to the King that I am marrying two girls from his palace? If he likes it, some people from the palace would not like it at all. In this case, I have to be very careful and continue to be loyal to our King and not to spoil the relationship we have built because of this insignificant girl.

***

Chapter Twenty-Three

Chief Hunter

After the dinner, I asked Tes for my kola nuts, pipe and a cup full of palm wine from yesterday's leftover drinks. Instead of her going inside and getting it like she would normally do, she called Si to get the drinks and the pipe for me, while she went to get the kola nuts. "Please my lovely, don't get drunk tonight. I beg you, just a little would be suitable, you understand?" Tes said. I did not want any argument, so I got on with my mischief. "That was all right, Tes," I said to her. She turned back and gave me kiss, "Yours always," she said to my left ear. She went in to bed.

Si came to tell me it was OK. She sat down on her previous seat and was looking at the sky, I knew not, that a few hours ago, she had went inside and put on some of the perfume Tes used to wear and washed her mouth. She became so radiant. I could not compliment this gesture because Tes might not be properly asleep. She knew I liked the idea, but as she was looking into the sky, telling me about the moon. I could see the two nipples pointed out under her tilted body cover. I used both hands to pull the nipples, she smacked my hand and said, "Get off, my aunt hasn't slept yet. You must behave yourself. Could I have a taste of your kola nut?" she said. I gave her a piece, which she put in her mouth at once, before I said no, she already started to chew it. "It's sweet."

"Yes, of course, why do we chew it if is not sweet?" Saying that she found herself seated down between my two legs with her back to me. This enabled me to get a hold of her breasts and stroke my right hand down and I touched her vagina. She was motionless, unable to move or say a word, all she was eager to do was to lie down. I didn't want that. I took my gberi garment off, and she could see my penis long and strong; I asked her to sit on it. She was almost crying and unable to breathe out when it was going inside her body. Her aunt was asleep close by, so she tried to whisper into my ears, "I am feeling the it in my stomach and I want it out."

"No that was a good feeling," I said. I got up and I asked her not to let it come out and that she should just lean on the basket table with her two hands while I stood at the back, which she never had before. She almost cried out loudly, until I shot it inside her.

"What a great relief!" she emphasised and gave a great welcoming smile. I could see she either wanted more or was looking for a chat. "I'm in the mood for a chat," I quickly said. I became wary and got an emotional feeling for my wife. I chose my words carefully, so she wouldn't understand my emotions. So many questions eroded my mind to be asked, but I could not spit them out, else she would feel I did not enjoy her. I tried to answer as much as possible the questions she asked and giggled when was I supposed to or smiled to whatever needed to be smiled at.

"Dear Chief, when would you like me to go home?" she asked. Exactly, one of the questions I vividly wanted to ask her which I thought could bring out contempt, so I paused.

"Tes did not want me to go back home; in fact, she said that I should ask you," she continued.

"Is that so?"

"Yes," she said, "Chief, I must go back because I do not want to get pregnant, neither should I challenge my cousin. What I have wanted, I have got it."

"And what is that?" Chief asked.

"Don't you know that nowadays most women won't give in to unsociable men; we want men of power and strong, Chief!"

"Yes," I said, "but what would happen if you are already pregnant now?"

"Never," she replied.

"So you just wanted me to remove the virginity for you, is that so?" I shouted.

"Yes," she said, and briskly she disappeared inside the house. I knew I had been used by a little girl.

"Come back here, you should never leave me whenever I am talking to you. Understand, you understand?"

"Yes Chief," and she went inside the house to sulk. I followed her and brought her out tenderly. She smiled and winked at me; she was pretty to an extent but not as pretty as Tes. However, I didn't feel like having an affair with her anymore; she is a user, and I could be a sucker to her love and that is what most of them wanted from rich men.

"When would you like to go home?" I asked her.

"I would like to go tonight."

"Positive, you got it."

"Dear Chief, are you fed up with me?"

"No, no, I just thought you needed to go; moreover, you will be able to provide us more information about the palace."

"You are a mind reader, dear Chief, "that was exactly what I was about to say!" she said in a surprised tone of voice.

"Probably, Tes wanted you to stay with her because of the festival."

"Exactly," she said, "dear Chief, if you don't mind, let me go and pack up my things."

"You can wait till the afternoon before you go, as you don't need to rush, and I am positive Tes would support my idea wholeheartedly."

She responded, "Yes, it is like husband and like wife. I hope to find a husband exactly like you."

"You have found him."

"You?" she asked.

"No, no, no, not me my Little Hunter," said Chief.

"He is too little for me."

"But, he is wise and famously known."

She giggled, knowing not what the future would be.

***

Chapter Twenty-Four

Chief Hunter

I was awakened by the sound of the voice of my Little Hunter greeting Tes and her cousin; he was asking for me. I was in bed half awake and half asleep; my decision was to sleep on and let Tes handle the situation.

I was awakened by Tes, who came to the bed and joined me in sleeping. She pressed her bottom to my pelvis. I threw my right hand across her shoulder and got hold of her right breast's nipple. I gently gripped her breast, which was a handful, caressing her as I usually did. It wasn't long before I shot it inside her.

As soon as we finished, we both hugged each other and went down into the shower room. It was not the first time we would shower together anyway. She washed me, and I washed her body tenderly.

"Darling Chief, what is wrong? It was unusual that I touched you but got no response from you. This is strange." She tried again and again but it never got strong, it just stayed weak and asleep. She was not happy.

"Probably I'm tired." I thought something was wrong because as soon as she touched me, I was supposed to become hard.

"You may need to drink some of your tonic which you prepared with the native herbs and dried leaves, which are specially brewed."

"Tes, nothing is wrong, I'm just too tired. Remember, I came inside you more than three times this morning; it was enough to make a man tired." She argued as if she knew what went on between me and her cousin.

I wouldn't say a thing about it, no matter how hard she pressed; she will never hear anything about it from me, I promised myself, except if she heard from her cousin. This was the first time I saw her getting upset and angry. "Are you OK?" I asked her.

"Just leave me alone and go your way," she replied.

I dressed up and said to her, "See you later." With no words from her, I went out on my way to visit my Little Hunter. I knocked on his door but got no response. As I turned the handle, the door easily opened. "Hello, hello ho, ho, ho."

"Woo, woo, woo, my Chief. I am very sorry, I just about to catch some sleep."

"Well, I was passing by and just wanted to say hello to you."

"Have your seat, Chief." Quickly he went to bring kola nuts and a pipe and the palm wine.

"I just got this wine down this morning, so Chief, be careful to push it."

"What' going on inside there?"

"My Chief, I saw Si to the palace and she apparently came to see me."

"Where is she?"

"Si, you don't need to hide anymore, you can never keep something from my Chief," Little said.

"So, Si you've been here already or how long ago?"

"Not so long, Little said I should come and help him out, with cooking and stuff," she replied.

"That was all right," I said. Of course, she could understand me, but Little was a pig in the middle.

"My Chief," Little called, "I was just expressing myself with Si about how I am going to make her a great husband, if she ever marries me. She, however, is doubting my integrity."

"Si, come here," I said. She came and knelt down in front of me. "You see, Little Hunter, he is right. I do not want to put my mouth into this matter, but since he called me, what I suggest you should do or both of you should do is to watch each other for some time and see how the love grows in between both of you, then you can both determine what you want."

"My Chief, I really love her so much."

"What about her? Is she in love with you? So, you have to give it some time to grow on both sides. Please, I allow you to rise up and go," I said. I wondered to myself how he would feel inside her? I just finished with her this morning, and am I in a position to give her out to somebody who is a friend of mine, what would happen if he knew in the future that I have been there? I may be disrespected and become a nuisance. There was no emotion from her face about this morning; she was getting on as normal. This made me very embarrassed and sad inside, but as well, very impulsive in doing something important for Little.

Giving her away made me feel good inside. This joy I took home to meet my sad wife. I thought she would not welcome me but as I knocked on the door, she opened with a thousand kisses. "Where did you go to? I have been thinking of following you but I could not guess where you would be. Then I sat down miserably till you came."

"I went to Little Hunter, who said I should give the leg of an antelope to you. What a nice little man he is! He always remembers me. I think one day you are going to be his aunt-in-law."

"Why?"

"Because the two have eyes on each other, although Si does not know yet, but the Little Hunter was so much in love and was trying to make her see it."

"How?"

'He brought her home to cook for him."

"I hope he has not been messing up and having an intercourse relationship with her?"

"I do not think so, Si was in the kitchen cooking and Little was about to sleep when I went in to see them. Therefore, nothing obvious happened between them."

"Why are you so upset with me?" Tes spoke frankly and hugged me and dropped her head unto my shoulder.

"Well, you requested for it, and that was the main reason I had to leave home and go to my friend." She was filled with apologies and asked for my forgiveness. She used certain words which always make me to forgive and forget all mistakes she might have made.

She said, "You know that I have no father or mother whom you could simply report me to for discipline and I have taken you as my father and mother as well as given my life to you. Do whatever you like to me. I will be sober and do according to your wish." She repeated these words again and I was fidgety and gave her a bear hug. Silently, we kissed, and I took my wife inside and we both played and had a good laugh. She prostrated and I carried her with me to the bed, and there we stayed and talked and kissed and laughed and we forgave each other.

***

Chapter Twenty-Five

Chief Hunter

"Chief, the Ogun festival is just in few months away," Tes said.

"No, it is more than that," I replied.

"I will keep my mind there; do not let it be too late for our preparation."

"OK, my pretty."

"What, what did you call me?"

"Of course, you heard me, *'my pretty one'*."

"No, no, do not call me that, I do not want to be big-headed."

"Tes, listen to me, occasionally I call you whatever I like, and you should answer me the same way, and I do not want you to be so subdued towards me. I want you to be proud and be as tall as I am. Then I will be able to respect and cherish you."

"Thank you, my love."

"Between you and me, I must let you know that this year the festival is going to be too exciting, simply because our King is unwell and, I don't want to depress you, but things were not as expected. Generally, there has not been much feeling of enthusiasm about it. Some people could not even face me or look me in the face and talk about it, like my Deputy. They kept sending people to me or to the palace to know my intention; is that good?" She paused not knowing what to answer back. Then I quickly dashed outside, and I could hear her voice in the distance. "No matter what, we are going to do it in my own way," she shouted sarcastically, "everyone is going to enjoy it!"

Tes started counting the days to know the actual festival date so it could be well planned for. Roughly eight to nine and a half months ahead. *She was always right*, I said to myself. Tes would need to call meetings with a few important women for support and generosity. The Deputy Head's wife was our senior lady; she was the eldest, knowledgeable, supportive and helpful but when it came to cooking, she was a little bit backward. It is not that she cannot cook but she was too old-fashioned. Tes dressed up and got ready to go and meet friends.

"Where are you going?" I asked.

"Darling, I need to meet some friends regarding the festival; you know I cannot do it on my own."

"But you need to do that when we are less busy, I suppose?" I said. Tes really wanted to do things by herself these days, so she went on her own way

I tried to recap what had been happening so far with a few pieces of kola nuts and my tobacco pipe in my mouth. As I was grinding the kola with the left molar teeth, likewise I was blowing the blue smoke, making onion rings into the air. I felt so relaxed, as if for the first time I was having time off work. Nothing much to think about except Tes's cousin and flashback to my relationship with her, how enjoyable and exciting that relationship was. I did not think much, when I caught sight of my bante swelling up so hard. If Tes was around, she could have redeemed the afternoon graciously. All I wanted was sex, sex and sex from my woman.

In fact, she was getting used to this. On some occasions, she would cuddle me and say softly, "Let us go to bed, I am feeling it badly and I need you." We would go and do it to the mutual satisfaction of one another. Briskly, I had a nap and when my eyes opened again, there was a completely different thought in my mind. That is, where, when and what about the festival; it's time for me to get prepared.

Every day, every time and every second of my thoughts were about the festival, my mind felt reluctant about doing anything. Looking around me, most men of my age had got three, four or five children, and I had no dream of having a pregnant wife, talk about having a child. So, I always dropped the subject of the festival in to a conversation and if there was drink, I would drink it off and forget about our childless problem.

There was a day I got drunk while thinking about my life. Tes was a lady I was so much in love with and wondered why she could not give me a child. Some of my friends already said probably she was not my wife, some people even said until I leave her for another woman, I would not have a child. I have done it with her cousin yet nothing has happened, I anticipated to hear a story from the palace about Si, my wife's cousin, getting pregnant but there was nothing. Therefore, it must have been my fault, unable to impregnate a woman.

Flashback to the beginning of my manhood; the first lady I had sex with was remarkable and fantastic and we had a very unusual kind of sex that one should have in their life.

Chapter Twenty-Six

Chief Hunter

I was in the bush one evening after having walked a long distance without finding any animal to kill. I killed one antelope, some of which I had for dinner, and then cut the rest of it into pieces and put in my bag. While looking forward, I saw a light that showed there was a hut. I reckoned I was not too far to a village or a village was not too far to where I was. I started to follow this light.

As I got nearer, I saw a lady who dressed like a chieftain's princess daughter. She wore beads with different colours around her head; at the centre of the beads on her forehead was a small cowry. There was a piece of cloth which covered her breast and a tight skirt that fell over her bottom. Of course she rolled the top of her breast to the left to make the cloth hold strong on her body. She stood at the doorway to the entrance of their hut, it seems she was conversing with someone seated down in front of her, whom I could not see. While I continued walking, she would stare at me and our eyes would cross and she would continue talking as well as staring at me and doing whatever she was doing.

Until I reached an opened field, she still stood by the doorway; it seems there was nobody there she was talking to, just fantasy. "Hello," I said to her, "it was a hot evening," but got no reply. She was living in a hut made of palm tree leaves and bamboo to make the hut strong and difficult for water or rain to penetrate.

"Hello," I said again.

"What do you want?"

"I came to see you, in fact to cheer you up."

"Do I actually request for somebody? No."

"I was tracing the light that I saw, it seemed someone was over there and of course, it would be too ridiculous if I passed through and did not say hello. After all, I am hunter, you may need my help," I said.

"Come inside," she offered me a kola nut and a smoke. I kept the kola nut in my side pocket and pretended I was chewing it. I blew the smoke she gave me unto her face; the gesture was not missed. Suddenly, she dropped the tight skirt. All that remained was the piece of cloth to cover her breasts. Her hair was black and shining as a replica of Tes' hair. She was lighter in complexion than Tes, of about 5ft 3ins tall. Her two breasts had very sharp nipples, much more pointed than Tes and Si's nipples. You must be careful looking into her eyes, they seem to cause extreme fear. I can hardly look. No matter how strong you are, you will have to look down. An immediate glance I had showed me she was aged. *I am not afraid of you*, I said to myself. I grabbed her and ripped the cloth off her chest and got the right breast into my mouth and squeezed the left one. Her nipples became very strong and I knew she's ready for me.

My whole body trembled in ecstasy and it was my first experience having sex with a lady so incomparably beautiful. Looking into her eyes was irrevocably disastrous because I did not know what I was seeing. Whether human, animal, demon or a freak animal. I didn't know; but something was actually dragging me to her. When she had finished packing another tobacco pipe, she passed it to me for smoking. I pulled the pipe once then I didn't know how, but I was on top of her and ejaculating as hard as possible until I went into her with a deep penetration. This extreme joy she could not handle, about to reach her orgasm she screamed with ecstasy and disappeared from my sight.

I saw lightning fire going around in the hut. Within three to five minutes, the whole hut, her belongings, the lights and lightning suddenly disappeared. I found myself in a bush field, seated down with surprise and anguish. I looked down below and saw my dick dripping of spasms and not as strong as he used to be, mainly because of the anguish. I took my sack, my rod, gun bow and arrow, stood up and looked around me, yet I didn't know her name or who to call for. I felt I should shout and call her but my mind refused to do so. I stood there and suddenly shouted, "Where are you, you, you, you?" My voice echoed through the darkness. I just wondered where she had disappeared to, I didn't know what to say, neither did I have someone to talk to about it.

If she didn't enjoy it, she could have talked to me, I said to myself, *then we could have repeat and do it again*. I shouted again, "You are a coward!" She is a coward, I said, and I should forget all about it and go on my way. I went back on my own way, hunting as much animals as I could. I only got another rodent to kill and then headed to my hut. I never thought of this lady, never had a flashback to what I did with her, whether it was immoral or if I had felt something disgusting in her, never. I could only believe it's part of growing up and being a man.

I, therefore, was attributing this to my failures for child making; I don't know. *Do I need to talk with someone about it?* The answer was NO. I have to live with it and let nature take its course.

***

Chapter Twenty-Seven

Chief Hunter

All the hunters were supposed to come and meet me, and we would discuss how and what we are going to do, and this should happen at least a week before the Ogun festival. Initially, I sent word to the palace for the date but I have still not received any response back from them, which means our King was not well and we might have to postpone or stop the whole ceremony. I could go on with the festival by undermining the King and continue without too much ceremony, which means there would be no dancing, drumming and killing a large animal for celebration.

However, I went to the palace myself to see the King. He was actually expecting me and as soon as he heard it was me, he said, "Come inside come inside, my Chief." He was welcoming me from the doorway. I was about 5ft away and I danced and shook my bum and threw him my hand. He said, "The man of war, that is the way you are." We shook up and down three times and dragged each hand till it clicked and then took it to the forehead, mouth and to the chest and punched each hand against one another. He was glad, and I felt so glad that he was alive and back in business.

"My Chief," he called me, "much would not be done this year. I am going away on a long journey and you will need to come here often and look after my home. This is about the ordination of another crown in one town named Shmile. We would be there for seven days; therefore, you can do your festival. By right you're supposed to follow me but because of this Ogun festival, you need to wait as the two of us should not be away at the same time."

He requested for his wife to bring me some kola nuts, which we would eat and chew together before I started my journey home. We both greeted each other the same way for departure, and I wished him a safe journey to Shmile. I knew he would go there with some of his helpers and most likely his Deputy, if there would not be many assignments for him to do. He occasionally travelled with his wife; she usually engaged in different activities.

By the time I reached home, Tes had been waiting to see me. "Ho, ho, darling you are welcome. Are you all right?" she asked.

"Fantastic, how about you?"

"Very well, thank you," she said.

"I missed you", I said, "this time."

She came forward to me and rubbing her hand on my face, kissed me and said, "I missed you too." I lifted her up and put her on my leg, and we both kissed each other; obviously, we were very much in love with each other.

"For your information, I have been to the palace. The festival will be on, and we can do as much as we would like, but I still feel reluctant to do much."

"Does not matter," said Tes, "after all, there would be more festivals to manage in the future. We still have the

Hunters Festival. So just forget about whether you are doing much or not and let the nature of festival take its course, like you used to say." We both looked at each other and burst into laughter and kissed the argument goodbye.

Tes said, "I have been to your Deputy's house to see his wife about the women's preparation for the Ogun festival. Your Deputy was there, and they both send their regards. I went there with Si, my cousin."

"Where is Si now?"

"She has gone home; of course, she is coming over tomorrow and staying till the end of the festival. Would that be OK for you?"

"Splendid, that would speed up whatever you wanted to do."

"Indeed," said Tes.

I don't know what was pressed in my mind or touched that brought me to the farmhouse. I disappeared again. Of course, I like it and sometimes I often feel I should be well-prepared and get all my gears ready for something like that. But, Tes may not like that I have disappeared or she might feel I did not take something important with me. Looking at my surroundings at the farmhouse, I knew the reason why I had to come to farm immediately. It was more than one reason; as I was sitting down, I could feel a lot of breeze coming from somewhere, so I went to the bedroom, and I found the place damaged. Part of the wall by the right side had been knocked down and the footsteps sold him out to me as the elephant that destroyed it last time. He had done the same thing again.

Due to them being herbivores, all the meats we had cooked and those we had buried in the ground were destroyed by them stepping on the meat place. The smell of the meat seems something they can eat, but they play with it. The fruits, bananas, plantains, kola nuts in their shells and the sugar cane we had gathered for the Ogun festival were all destroyed and eaten by the elephants. I stood there in amazement; anyone seeing me would have laughed their heads out of their necks, to see that the proud Chief Hunter made such a blatant mistake, not protecting my farm and property with full security. I felt disappointed. Without hesitation I got all equipment I needed out and started to do the job, because I didn't want anybody to see it, nor Tes to worry.

***

Chapter Twenty-Eight

Chief Hunter

As I was building the wall, I put pepper in the mud. The water I used to mix the mud was so pepper rich that from about two to three miles away you would be able to smell the pepper. Generally speaking, this would deter elephants and make them run away from my farmhouse and my farmlands. They would even change their path to somewhere else because of the smell of the pepper. Moreover, I moved my room to the other side of the house because elephants never forget their routes, and nothing, nothing could ever disturb or prevent them from going on their own way.

The farmhouse had only one bedroom before; this time I increased it to two and put more amenities inside to accommodate visitors, and made it more modern, even better than the house we lived in in the town. I could not finish the job, it seems I would need to continue tomorrow; therefore, I should have a break. I decided to go to a hut near my plantations and see what they have done. Ho, ho, ho it was not the elephant that did these, it was the bush pigs and piglets. The corn/maize farm was intact, nothing bad happened to them, only the yam, coco, and cassava plantations were damaged a little bit. *Probably, the elephants drove them away, else they could have destroyed the farm.* But how do I know this? I could vividly see them, their footsteps and the elephant's fiercest movement showed me.

So, I delayed my rest till tomorrow because it's normal to do planting in the evening time so that the moisture of evening could relax what you are planting and the soil would breathe into it to make it grow much better. I went into the shed and took my cutlass and hoe, planted more and more yams, cassava and coco yams, more than what I had got before. This time I made the farm much bigger, the way I had always wanted it to be.

I was so tired and now felt like seeing my wife, I missed her. She would have accompanied me, singing for me, made my food and put water in the bath shed for me while I was working. I have already put some coco yam and cassava into the fire buried in the ground. By the time I finish, they would be well done and ready to eat with the rodent, which I have stuffed pepper and garden eggs inside. I felt so tired; neither could I fetch water to bathe or drink. Luckily, I had some water in the farm shed.

I struggled but I got up and got the water and food, which I had just cooked, and ate a good dinner. It was so delicious that I could not leave anything till tomorrow for my breakfast. I also had a good drink of water mixed with palm wine found in the farm shed and took the whole keg into the farmhouse for my enjoyment, but I could not finish the wine.

When my eyes opened, it was the morning. I had nothing on my mind than to wash my face and to continue with my job in the farm. As I had entered the farmland to inspect what I had done, I actually saw some of the pigs. I ran after them and they ran away. So they had made my farm their dining palace? OK, OK, OK, I said and went to get all the traps that could catch them both alive and dead. I set them on both the entrance to the farm and inside, to catch as much as I possibly could. I had to do it early because the bush pigs and piglets fed both days and nights; they don't know when to stop feeding.

I went towards the building, also inspecting what I did yesterday. A fantastic job! I praised myself, knowing not that my angel was already in the living room, taking care of everything that was not properly done. As I went to take a short rest inside, before starting today's work, I saw Tes coming out to fetch me.

"You are always promising you will take your kits with you whenever you go out. What about these? Chief, I beg you, never forget to take your rod, batten and your bow and arrow, especially when coming to the farmhouse."

"Tes darling, I know, many thanks."

"I know you are strong but to some people you are not."

"Exactly," I said, "many thanks to you." I drew her closer and we both cuddled for a while. We had really missed each other; all was completely silent. I gripped her two legs, raised them up and gave a deep, deep penetration, I looked up at her face to see if what I was doing met with her satisfaction. To my surprise, she was crying. I stopped and asked, "Why? Aren't you enjoying it?"

"I am, I am; please do not stop, just carry on," she urged.

Excitement and sadness both came to me at once. *I had to stop,* but she hugged me tightly.

"No answer to my question?" I continued.

"Did you ask one?"

"No, I didn't." She got her towel out and started to wipe and dry my body.

"Splendid," I said, "and thank you."

Then she knelt down on both knees and said "Thank you, my husband, I love you." She swallowed some of it and used the rest to rub her face. Her face was whitish as if she put a powder on.

"Isn't that disgusting?" I said.

"No, it is my emblem of love and it makes your face look young."

"How did you know that?"

"It is medicinal advice from my parents." She wiped my back dry again and my face too. Without any hesitation, I dashed out of the room.

***

Chapter Twenty-Nine

Chief Hunter

As I looked up to the sky, I reckoned it might start to rain later on. I hoped I could push this job to a certain extent so that I would not be afraid if it rained. I continued with the ball of sands and stones mixed with pepper and putting them one by one on top of each other and at the front side till she came outside. "Chief, you have demolished the place, have you, and rebuilding it to your taste. Why do like to give yourself so much headache? Can't you sit down without working?"

I smiled back at her, "When I stop working, that is when I die." She became a good helper by throwing moulded balls of sand to me. As the balls were about to finish, I came down and moulded more balls. Within two to three hours, we finished with the walls, and I must not let it be too dry before I put the rafters in. I don't want the flat roof which some animals would be using as their nest, and a lion or cheetah or leopard may find it easy to climb and make the roof their hiding place. I went to the bush and got some woods and ropes from the banana tree. First of all, I built a ladder which enabled me to get to the top and down and then made another one for Tes so she could be able to help me up and down. We could not finish the work as it started to rain.

Suddenly, I heard the sound of the pigs crying as though a trap had caught them. I ran down the farmland. As I was about to run past Tes, she said, "Have you taken your weapons with you?"

"Tes, it is just down in the farm." She still went to get me my long rod, batten, and the native gun which I made for my use. "Please don't follow me behind so soon, because of the wild animals," I cautioned. As soon as I moved closer to them, the male was running towards me fiercely. I will not back down for this, I said, and I switched the long rod into my right hand as he was coming. When he was about a hundred yards from me, I raised up the long rod. He was about to hit my left leg when I used the rod on his head and towards the back end of his neck. His head was smashed into pieces and only the skin that protected it stopped it spreading everywhere. It was the male trying to protect the female and the piglets which had almost reach the standard age of consumption.

Those ones caught by the traps were crying savagely for salvation. I moved closer to the other big one which I thought was a female and used the rod on her head. Instantly, she died. Gently, I released the two piglets, put ropes on their necks and dragged them to the farmhouse, and I told Tes to go and get the kills which I had made very close to the farm, near the yam and cassava plantations. She was overjoyed and ran back saying, "Chief, Chief, I could not lift any or carry them, they are just too much heavy for me to drag." That was when I realised how big they were. Quickly, I dashed off and brought them inside to be cleaned for later consumption.

Now we needed division of labour. Either I concentrated on looking after the kills or continued with the building work. You know as a female they would always prefer to do cooking, rather than muscular work. Well, I don't hesitate either way. In fact, I would have preferred her to be doing the cooking, then I would be focused on the building. She didn't care for this division and instead she randomly disturbed me as I was doing this strenuous work; I tell you it's amazing how she makes me bang my head or bang the hammer on my fingers.

I was using the stone to bang the wooden pegs in to the roof as she was staring at me. I knew instantly that she was staring. You know when one is staring at you and you are using a little bit of the corner of your eye to see it? As I wanted to look back at her, I wedged the stone on my fingers which I was using to hit the peg. The stone fell away from my hand and water was about to drip down from the eyes. It was painful. Before I started dancing around in agony, she put the three fingers inside her mouth as if her mouth would numb the injured place. Although, it calmed the pain down a little bit, she would not let go of the fingers for the next thirty minutes. That was the required time you had to put it in the mouth if you wanted to ease the pain. I learned that for now. "You must be enjoying my fingers remaining in your mouth," I said.

"It's only me who knows what I was doing with your fingers. It's not easy to put a dirty hand in your mouth, you know. It is sickness and you can only do it for someone you love." I went quiet and continued with my work.

I went around to inspect what I had done so far, to adjust and make corrections where necessary, putting finishing touches where necessary. It didn't take much time from me and everywhere was looking good and I would expect people to praise me for the good work well done.

As I was going up the ladder to continue doing the good job, I heard the crying again of the piglet. I jumped off the ladder, ran within the vicinity and I could see the mother running up and down. I stepped back a bit after having a look and planned my next action because bush pigs aren't something to be messing about with. One bite from your body cannot heal forever because they would pour sickness into you. A bite they take would tear the skin from the bottom to the top, and it would continue eating until you die. But if you drive them away, they would run but would come back again. They don't give up easily, when they get food.

However, I could see the piglet mum trying to get the baby released from the trap using her nose, digging the ground to get rid of the trap, but luckily enough it was too deep. I cocked my gun; it was a while since I had used it. I pointed it at the big female bush pig and pulled the trigger, it went dead. The rest of piglets ran away and the piglet caught by trap was already dead, and I carried the two back, with Tes following me behind witnessing all my actions.

***

Chapter Thirty

Chief Hunter

"My Chief, there is a big dinner tonight," she said. "I would like to get back to the town and get my cousin Si to come to help. What do you think, Chief?"

I could have suggested that she should not worry because we would be getting to town tomorrow, but she felt so excited. "You seem to be very happy," I asked jokingly.

"Because you are doing very well, you are a strong man and I admire you so much. I love it, love it and I love it!" she exclaimed. "Look how many bush pigs you have killed today and we even got live piglets in our nursery! How many live animals have we got now? We have got six different species, goats, pigs, dogs, tortoises, chickens and turkeys. Thank you, Chief," she was saying till we reached the farmhouse.

Instantly, I went back to my work and continued with the roof till I was about half way done. Tes kept calling and yelling, but I did not answer her. "I had told you do not try to do everything by yourself, leave it till we reach home, when you have got lot of hands to help you out," I said.

"Don't you know I need to do something by myself as a skilful woman?" She carried on as if nothing was wrong, and no more shouting for help. For the next two to three hours, there was extreme quietness. I was able to finish the roof and was left with the door and window, which I created in our new parlour. "Another one or two hours might bring us to the finishing of the building," I told Tes.

"Come on, let us see the end result. I will not disturb, but be a good helper to you," she replied. So, we continued and she was assisting me, working like a man. I knew she could do it. By the time I told her we had already finished, she could not believe it, we held each other, sat down to relax our muscles and had something to drink. That was when I realised that it was fantastic weather; the day was full of breezes and sunshine.

Tes went inside and brought out the leftover palm wine and some kola nuts, some of which she was hoarding in the farm for selling in the market. She wanted me to have taste and to see if they were ready for selling. Of course, palm wine and kola nuts would definitely make a good afternoon. I tasted and gave her feedback, it was remarkable. "Could you please get my smoke pipe, darling?" I requested.

"Ho yes, ho yes Chief," she responded and went inside for it. She was now settled down, preparing her cooking as well as roasting some meat for our dinner.

"This time, Tes, you must try as much as possible to take whatever you are capable of taking that you may or would need at home with you, because we are going to stay for a while before we come back to the farmhouse. Of course, I would be coming on and off due to the Ogun festival and the market days for the hunters," I said.

"How would you protect the crops and the farmhouse, because of animals that walk over our house, like elephants?" she asked.

"Well, I've built it with more security protections this time. I can promise we will never be disturbed by elephant or any other wild animals in this village house again." So, we both started packing. I was delighted because we had got more than enough kills to celebrate the festival as well as to sell at the market. Women usually knew what they were taking to the market to sell and what was required for upkeep.

I reckoned it must be between the fourth and fifth hour of the morning. "I think I want some now," she whispered in to my ear. We rolled up and down the bed several times, enjoying the opulence of the morning. She got up and I said, "Don't try to put any water in the bath. When I reach home, I will bathe. Let us wash our faces and go." We both quickly washed our faces and set on our way to the town. I felt like disappearing to our house in the town but what about the stuffs we are carrying? Instantly, she looked up at my face, probably she felt the same way, so I cuddled her. "Are you all right?" I asked, "What are you contemplating?"

"Nothing, I just felt heavy and tired."

"We shall soon reach home."

We crossed all areas where there could be problems but nothing happened. I was glad because I always don't want any problems whenever she is with me, or when we are going out together. As soon as we reached home, I put everything where it was supposed to be, took her shoes off and carried her to the bed. Then I made a little fire to keep the kills warm till they could be properly taken care of when she woke up. We both slept for several hours.

A lot of people came knocking on the door but got no response. Then Si came in. I seemed to briefly awaken but still could not answer her. She must have gone back I thought. It was exactly in the afternoon, when we awoke. She gave me a kiss and it was a succulent one, then we led each other to the bath shed. "I have not prepared the water bath," she said.

"OK." I sat down on a little stool until it was ready, and then we bathed together. I was in the room when I overheard the two of them discussing. "So I was right to have seen Si?" I later asked Tes.

"Yes, she even told me you greeted her very well," Tes replied.

"Did I? I cannot even remember that."

"Why?"

"She's up here early."

"Of course, Chief," she said, "she hasn't got anywhere to go to. Moreover, if she stayed at the palace, she will be overworked."

"Ah, I see she is your faithful cousin and friend."

***

Chapter Thirty-One

Chief Hunter

I noticed that she did not like me calling Si her friend, she didn't want me to emphasise about whether they like each other or not. I have to close that chapter.

The day after tomorrow is the hunter's market day and as always, three days after that would be the Ogun festival. Today's cooking had been well done, I ate as much as I would like to eat but it would have been much better to see a boy or a girl to share it with. I was not loud about it; therefore, she could not hear me but she kept looking at my face. Neither could she be distracted from looking my face – when she was asleep, she often knew I was around her or felt my presence around her.

On the market day, we are the first to open the market stall. Tes and Si were both busy throughout and made lot of money. Including all the animal skins, they sold everything they went to the market with and came back very early, before lunch time.

I could see she was exceedingly happy and content, this made me happy and we started to continue with our preparation for the festival and were joyful for the rest of the evening.

I am now sceptical whether I should send an invitation to our colleagues in neighbouring towns, since it is not going to be elaborate. So I withheld my invitations and just thought if they came or not, it would all be well and good. Of course, they would understand that if there was a need, I would have sent them an invitation. In this case, obviously nothing was going on.

The cooking was going steadily. I only saw my wife when our eyes met. "Chief," she called, "please wait for me," and instantly I waited. Some of your friends or colleagues have been dropping some killings, especially your Little Hunter he has been in twice today, but was always met with your absence."

"Don't they request to see me?"

"They all wanted to see you but when you are not in, I cannot say much to let them stay because I am really busy."

"OK, I do understand, thank you very much, you can now go back to your business."

"Can you please give me a kiss?"

"Is that all you want?"

"Yes, as of now." Smoothly, I gave it to her and went on my own way.

"Could you please send Si to get Little Hunter for me for an errand?"

"OK, I will," she responded and went away. It was not too long before Little Hunter came in. As you know, he must keep the tradition going, he has to greet me as usual for seeing me well and healthy. He has to shake his bottom because it is the shaking of bum and tail that a dog uses to salute and greet its breeder.

"Well, I am on to preparing for the 'God of Iron' Ogun Night, and you must make people understand that is not the Hunter Festival. 'Ogun' is before the Hunter Festival. So far you are the only person that came in, I'm expecting the rest of hunters to join in the preparation. They should not sit on their asses, expecting me to do everything for them," I said.

It wasn't so long before they started coming in one by one; in fact, I was surprised since it was like they happened to have heard that it is the time we should go to Chief Hunter. They even came with some of our favourite things, drinks and smokes and many others to make the evening pleasant for the God of Iron, 'Ogun'. The work was going on smoothly without any issues, I was very happy; directing my attention towards Tes, who suddenly came to see her golden boy Chief Hunter, I smiled. My Deputy signalled to Tes to keep all what we brought till tomorrow for the festival night. She called Si and Deputy Hunter's wife and started taking things inside. Some of the hunters lamented, "Where you taking our stuff to? These are meant for our use tonight."

"Ho no, no, no," Tes said, "not tonight, tomorrow night, you are mistaken."

The Deputy Chief said, "I think she is right; we do not need any drink tonight, but certainly tomorrow night we should drink and dance."

"Chief," he said, "we should have just a little to make our outing a bit sparkling." Before the Deputy said it, Tes had already left some palm wine and tobacco leaf for them to use. "Good wife," he said and blessed her. Under the tents we were drinking and laughing and making fun until the following morning.

The singing is what woke me and my wife up from bed. I didn't even know she slept with me. "Your water is in the bath, Chief. We would need to bathe quickly before people started coming in for the occasion." As usual we both went to bathe together. She rubbed my body with the great ointment of coconut oil mixture. Its perfume and shine declared to all that I was the Chief. Then we both put on the special clothing for the occasion. Of course, it was the one we wore last year. "Chief," she asked, "are we wearing this?"

"Yes, of course. I Chief Hunter do not need to show any feeling for new attire for the occasion, and we both look fantastic in it," I replied. The drum leader was using the big drum, calling my name and asking if I woke up well or not. I kept answering back, "I am well."

Tes responded, "He cannot hear you say that."

I knew, that was the part of the excitement, the joy of the festival occasion. I could not come out alone, I would need to come out with my wife to the high table. When the big drum called me, he would call my wife and give us information about people who had come in and those that had just been arriving.

"I don't need to rush myself. It's our day, even the King and heaven can wait," I said to my wife, and the drum leader said the same with his talking drum.

***

Chapter Thirty-Two

Chief Hunter

Give women the chance, they would take a thousand miles. Tes took all the time to dress up and I had nearly disappeared when she said, "I am ready now to come out." So, the Little Hunter went to inform the drummers we were on our way out now. They turned the drumming message saying that, "You are welcome, Chief and Mrs, you are both welcome."

I said, "Let the ceremony begin." Then the Little Hunter and Deputy Hunter came out to praise Ogun, the God of Iron, starting with incantations and then they got the permission from me to kill the dogs. Normally, they should kill about four to five dogs for the ceremony but because it's not a big festival, we killed two. Before the killing of dogs, there were two invitees from a nearby town. They came to greet me and brought us some kola nuts and a dog which we could not kill as it was reserved for next year. The Little Hunter selected some youths with himself to tidy up the killing and preserve it for cooking.

Breakfast was served in the morning, by eleventh hour, with pepper soup, and it depended on your choice. There were varieties to choose from – snake, chicken, beef, goat, turkey, lamb or dog soup. You had to tell them what soup you want with some bread.

The afternoon cooking contained rice, gari, eba, amala, pounded yam, or coco yam, or pounded plantain. These are called solid food. These were drunk with palm wine and sour wine, these were made from maize, and another with oka baba and sekete. The Ogun people began singing and others wanted to join in.

Around the third and fourth hour of the afternoon, I had to go around and greet people and pray and bless them for coming to our festival. We are supposed to go around three time, but I could not be bothered, and I only performed the dances which were very important for people to recognise you. I went around with Tes; she was blessed and received lot of gifts, both medicine and money.

The Little Hunter came out again, praying and blessing Tes while she was kneeling down for him. They were all happy and continued with their dancing, and Little Hunter asked Tes to get up and remain with blessing.

I later asked her, "It seems you receive a lot of medicine rather than money. Why and what for?"

She said all the medicine given to her was for her to get pregnant in good time and most of the blessings received are for her to get pregnant. "They love you too much, Chief," she exclaimed. People ate and took food home. The party stopped at twelfth hour of the night. Some who did not go to sleep were there till the morning and then went away.

"Chief, it was no small party. If you wanted to have a party, do it, because people would always turn out, they like you, especially if you are going to feed them for free, you will always get people to turn up. You are influential and accommodating and you love them and they love you. Hence, people would dance to your tunes," Tes said and we both slept afterwards.

It was the cockerel crow that woke me up. I was just thanking God that it was over and there was no problem with my wife or anybody or complaint from any angles; the Ogun festival was joyful and I can never forget it.

I felt giddy knowing not what to do, although my feeling was to be in the farm, but people would say why I cannot stay with my wife. I sneaked away by disappearing to the farmhouse, looked around everywhere and went to the plantation. Everywhere seemed to be OK. I came back to the farmhouse, looked around inside and outside. The house was OK, the way we left it and quickly I went back to sleep beside Tes.

"Your body is nice and cool," she said, "have you been outside?"

"Yes.

"To the farm?"

"No. I just went around the house outside."

"Of course, that is sufficient to keep you cool." She moved her body closed to me and held me tighter.

Suddenly, I fell asleep again. Another sound sleep that took me almost to the late afternoon, when I woke up to the sound of Si and Tes playing with each other. Si wanted to wake me up. Tes said, "No, I will wake my husband up. No one should wake him up for me," and she came and met me on the bed.

"Who was that?" I asked.

"Si," she said.

"Didn't she follow Little Hunter home?"

"She did not because we have got lot to do here. She knew that some of the women who have gone would still come back because a lot needs to be done to put the house in the way it was before," Tes replied. I could see how tired I was, we all need to sleep like that in order to remain healthy.

***

Chapter Thirty-Three

Chief Hunter

Suddenly, I remembered one of my old friends, the 'Chief Priest' Holy Man. In fact, it's been so long that I have seen him.

Without hesitation, I took my garment and as my second foot was about to come out of the house, I heard Tes calling, "Chief, Chief, Chief!" Three times she called. "Where are you going without anything, at least take your rods with you?" she said. "You cannot go out without anything to fight with." That was Tes' standard remark, especially with regard to my rod. Whenever she sees this with me, then she knows I am safe and ready to go anywhere. Without my rod, she would call me back and ask me to take it.

"You can't be going to see a friend in the east and taking just a little rod with you. Remember, you have to cross the market through the east side to the west before you reach the priest's house."

Of course, I don't like to cross the market sides, especially when the market was not on, it usually looked like ghost town. And that is why elderly people often say to children not to go to the market when market is off, simply because it's scary and has an evil haunt. However, I went back into the house, took my long rod, batten and sword and in my back hid the small native gun by wearing a shirt on top of it. Although it was swollen and visible that something was hidden in there, you hardly noticed it was my weapons. I let my mini waist skirt and 'Gberi-Ode' (long gown) cover it. This looked like a great discovery and new way of dressing up; of course, it's every day we learn. Not so long after I made my way, and I was there in time.

"Ago onile o, Ago onile o, Hello o, o, Hello o, o." I repeated it twice.

"Ago-ya, agoya o," the Chief Priest answered me twice. I was happy, the sound of his voice was eloquent quite impressive, a sound of safety, healthy and showing there was no problem with him. I shook my bum to the left and to the right three times, and we shook hands with a bear hug. He loved it and you could see the grin on his face. "What a long time since we've seen each other?" he said.

"How do you do?" I asked.

"I am very, very, well and thank you, my dearest Chief Hunter. How is my beautiful Tes, hope she all right?"

"Yes, we were all right."

"Thanking the God of Iron and Oracle," we both said.

"My Chief Hunter, today is the Oracle Day and from morning I have been receiving visitors from all over the place and I've been blessing people from morning and that was the way it is. The King had just sent his messenger, they left here some time ago. Those people you met when coming in are from the first lady of the town. The King's first wife."

"No, no, no, the first lady of the town is Iya Agan and the King's first wife was the second. How come people always mixed them together, you aren't the only person who did not know about this. In fact, lots and lots of people from this town do not know our first lady is Iya Agan."

"My Chief Hunter, you need to prostrate now for blessing," he ordered. He continued praying, "Just go in peace, may God always be with you, you have no problem."

"Are you sure?" I asked.

"Yes, I said go in peace. And I repeat, God is with you."

So, I sat down and said to myself, so God is with me, is it true? How come I am barren? I was disinterested. *No disrespect*, I said to myself, *he should know better that I have had long enough to have or rear child*. So I responded, "Yeah, it's been a long time." He smiled. I could not voice out what I intended to say, else he would have thought there was an issue. I expected him to know better and tell me what 'God' thought about me not having a child all these days or what God was going to do.

"Yeah, my Chief, it has been. I have been too busy, plus the drought that happened last year, it was remarkable event but let us be given thankful to God."

"Chief Priest, I think we should sometimes find ways to make it rain whether it likes it or not."

"Do you think we haven't tried? Several performances to make it rain. I'll tell you something, God does whatever he likes, and he is the only person you cannot force or move, question or harass for information. If he likes he can make afternoon be as dark as night or morning as afternoon or blooming night, whom are we to question him?

"We only try to make it rain, only, if he says yes. That is why we say we should try to do good so that God can forgive our wrongs. And I kept saying to people to do good. Please do good, my son, but woe to those who have ears," he finished.

So, I got up and said bye. I departed through the back door because of people who were still waiting to see him. Why the back door? Because I am one of the important people, I do not need to walk through the audience nor to be known or seen with common people. They may know how he came but how he left would be unknown. Similar treatments were given to the King and other important people.

***

Chapter Thirty-Four

Chief Hunter

As soon as I reached home, I told Tes, who immediately contacted the Deputy Chief's wife. They both went to see the Chief Priest at home. In appreciation of this, he would need to reciprocate the visit and come to our home and sit with us for an hour or two, as is custom when someone's wife visits him. When he does come around we would discuss about much more important things, such as politics, affairs about your family, your town and the city. In fact, the Chief Priest is the one and only one you can talk in confidence with and feel safe when he's with you. We generally believe he is a man of knowledge wisdom and is safe with your secrets.

When our wives go to see him, he would look after them like his own children or wives, give them the fatherly advice a woman needed to enjoy her marital life. No woman goes to visit him without becoming wiser when they return home; they become more feminine, respectful, loyal and lovely and affectionate with their husbands. The Oracle Chief Priest would also visit you at home to settle the ups and downs in the family. If it's monetary, he may offer a little help towards the solution of the major problem. Where the little help does not settle the problem, he would keep praying, even though most problems of this time are not monetary.

Where there is a deterioration in behaviour in either the man or the woman, he would tell you or make you understand this so you can amend it to see the joy of your relationship and prosper in the marriage you've entered into. As there were languages for every contractual obligation, so there are languages for married life. It is only where this language, '*sharing, understanding, tolerance and acceptance*' is too difficult to practice that you see the breakdown in marriage. Where one of them is missing, the marriage may be unsettling. Have you asked yourself if these four are present in your marriage? So, the Chief Oracle Priest would often advise. It seems no one paid particular attention to what he said; occasionally I do, but sometimes it was just too overwhelming for me to practise all his preachings. But when trouble occurs, that is when we do appreciate him, and he often refers you back to what he said to you last time and which you had forgotten.

Nobody pays his wages or salary, only God pays him for the marvellous work he does for the community.

The weather was so good; the fresh air was coming from the sea. I looked around with one eyelid up so she would not get the idea that I was looking for her. Our four eyes met each other, but she would not stop whatever she was doing and come to me lately, she would prefer me to come to her. *Why?* I asked myself. She was busy, as Si was plaiting her hair for her, I therefore accepted the way she behaved towards me and felt grateful. After all, men always believe their wife was plaiting their hair for them.

As soon as she came in, "Tes," I said, "I have been preparing to go to the bush and the farm." She paused. "Why pausing?" I asked.

"I want you to stay."

"No, you know all that work that must be done before the Hunters festival and we surely need to prepare."

"I cannot come with you," Tes said.

"No, do not worry, I got some killings, wine and my favourite fruits," I replied. She smiled with a good gesture and I winked. Si was about to go away. Tes went to the kitchen to get ready for the dinner. "I cannot see you too far," said Tes to Si.

"Anywhere would be all right for me," Si replied.

"Why didn't you wait for the dinner?" I asked Si.

"It would be too late, and I would not be able to go home. I don't want to fall asleep here."

Tes made some cassava starch 'fufu', which we ate with melon stew and chicken. She put four pieces of honeycomb as desert in a separate plate. "Have you ever tried this before, my Chief, after your dinner? I would like you to taste it before you chew your kola nut and smoke tobacco, OK?"

"OK." We both ate, filled up and had the honey afterwards; in fact, this made my digestion fast and easy and I was able to burp several times, evidence that I've had a good dinner. I could not chew any kola nuts or smoke tobacco before I drifted off. I was awoken by Tes saying it's time for me to go now. She had prepared for me some food and got all my gears ready to go to the farm.

***

Chapter Thirty-Five

Chief Hunter

"Moreover, Chief, you will need to help me carry some of the stuff to the farm."

"No, no, no, no, Tes, I told you never mix up these stuff with mine, I may lose them."

"OK, OK, I thought you would be able to help me."

"Very sorry, indeed I cannot."

"That is all right." I dashed out, it was half morning and half night weather, it was still dark though early. As I was going I put a few guinea pepper and kola nuts in my mouth, these made my eyes wide open and full of energy, making me wide awake. It was not so long after that I reached the stream where I used to swim and clean up in the morning. I felt a little peckish but my mouth needed to be cleaned. I got my chewing stick out of my sack, washed my mouth, cleaned my tongue, throat and gurgled it with water spat it away in the bush. I did this three times until I felt good. As I was swimming, I could see that a bit of fishing would do no harm. I came out of the water and took the arrow which I normally used for fishing. I got four big fish and thought this would be adequate for dinner, if not too much, then cleaned up myself and headed to the farmhouse.

The farmhouse was intact the way we left it before going to the town, except a couple of bowls Tes used to cover things which had fallen down in the kitchen. *Before I do a bit of farming, I really need to make some killings, antelopes, giraffe, or pigs,* I said to myself and headed to the bush to hunt. I went to the bush from midday. All I could see were uninteresting or unwanted animals; in fact, this made me return empty-handed. *It does happen!* I exclaimed to myself whilst in deepest thought of what I should have done or left undone in the bush, what I should have killed even when I felt it's too small. I should not come home empty-handed; it is no good sign at all. I tried and got myself out of deep thinking, and told myself to proceed with caution next time regarding what I should do and make no mistakes. I said, "No animal is too small or too big for a kill." Throughout the whole week it was absurd; farming may be more pleasant than going around the bush without luck.

Certainly not, I could not switch back to farming, it was not the season. This time last year the bush blossomed, hunting would be your favourite work. Yet, sometimes it could be devastatingly wrong in the bush, as I am experiencing now. These effects lasted three months, with me going up and down without any animal to kill. I prayed and killed a dog for the God of Iron to bless and support me, but there was still no change or sign that I would see an animal, from the cat family for example, to excite myself.

I had to go home now; I had been missing my wife. She did not contact me or send messages to me through our dog, pigeon, or the duck that used to come through the river behind our home. Well, I don't know whether she may feel the same way I feel. As I was about to enter the village, I met one little boy who said, "Hello, where are you coming this time, are you not supposed to be at home with your wife?"

"What is your problem?"

"She has been longing to see you."

"How do you know about this?"

"Because I went with my mom to see your wife and I am afraid she needs help."

"OK. Thank you," I said and he went. Soon I reached home and she was very happy. I could see she had put on some weight.

"How are you?" I asked.

"Yeah, I am up and down."

"What do you mean by that?"

"It is too much; I will tell you everything later. I would like you to relax first and feel at home before I raise your blood pressure."

"You'll need to tell me everything."

"Okay," she said and went away.

Knowing not, my wife had already conceived and she had been pregnant for well over three months. The last time I left her, she was actually vomiting. She said to me she had been coughing all night and didn't know where the cough was coming from. I had told her it was the cold weather and the early morning mist. You know, early morning and when going towards evening, we usually get this horrible cold weather that makes you cough. "Yeah," she said and that was how I left her at the house that time and appeared at the veranda outside our farmhouse breathing in the fresh air.

"I have just finish cooking your favourite food," Tes said as she went and put food on the table. She took the seat in front me and she was about to speak when I also started talking. "You first," I said.

"You first," she said.

"OK, have you ever seen me like this before?"

"How?"

"Having come back from bush without kills, nothing to eat or carry."

"No, no," said Tes.

"The bush has been too difficult for me, no killings, every day, day in and day out, even at night. Why? I don't know."

"Well, we have been killing all these days. I will try and make adjustment so that we do not run out of food," said Tes. Then she asked, "What about the meat I buried inside the house, are they there?"

"I did not touch them nor knew you saved some meat over there."

***

Chapter Thirty-Six

Chief Hunter's Wife, Tes

"What do you want to tell me?" he asked.

"Darling Big, I am pregnant," I said.

"What?" he fell backwards with a great shock. "No, you aren't," he replied.

"Yes, I am, Big."

"How did you find out?"

"Your Deputy's wife came here to see me and did some examinations while asking some questions. She figured out that I am pregnant." I opened my wrapper and asked him to put his palm on my belly. He did and felt some figure moving. I also felt it amazingly. I could not believe it.

"It's wonderful such new could cause chaos," he said. Chief started to lament, it seemed as though he was both joyful and sad. "Why did you suddenly pause? Why should our joy be sadness?" I asked.

"Because the forest has changed, the animal has moved out."

"To where?" I asked. "Recently, I met two of your colleagues' wives in the market, one of them told me her husband killed buffalo last week and she sends you the front leg. And, Little Hunter always sends you kills."

"When last did you hear from him?"

"Yesterday," I replied, "you have not allowed me to tell you what has happened in your absence."

"The vow I have committed myself into. I walked from morning to evening and absolutely found no animals for me to kill. Quite unusual. Why only me?" he asked himself aloud.

"Do people know you are pregnant yet?" he continued.

"I don't know, you should know better that some people will know but would not say it to my face, or confront me to ask if I am pregnant. Nobody. Our Hunters' festival is within two to three months' time. The baby is due in a month or two months' time if I am not mistaken," I said. "This is our mixed blessing from God. I do not know why on earth you promised to kill a tiger. Isn't that too much exaggeration?"

"Now you want answers to all the above questions?"

"Yes, darling," I replied, while we both were laying in each other's arms.

He said, "You have answered the first questions, it was my misfortune and I need to work harder."

"No, not harder but more, Chief," I exclaimed silently, "it is natural that something may be inadequate, especially in this period, we have to take things easy and accept what 'God' gives us. For example, your friends get kills and you do not, and the kills they brought you are fresh directly from the bush. It has always been the case and it is natural and the philosophy of life that whenever you are expecting important things in life, you are bound to lack or have inadequate amounts of something else. All we need is perseverance."

He lowered his head down to my mouth and gave me a kiss, "How did you know about this?"

"Because I know that life is mathematics $2+2+2-2 = 4$. You must sacrifice a cowry. So, I realised things should not go on smoothly like that, else the impact could be disastrous, which you and I would not like. Our answer is perseverance; moreover, you cannot please the whole wide world."

"This has answered some questions in my mind," he replied.

"Nothing changed in my mind about you, I love you dearly, and I preferred to die for you or before you," I continued, until Chief broke out saying, "before I left for the bush, I felt that you do not love me like you used to do. The affection and sexual feelings are not there anymore, why!"

"Ah, my mood might have changed. I should have noticed or become aware. The first time I pushed you out of bed, and you fell down on the floor, during my sleep, myself I felt it and asked, why? I did not want to smell you around me. Your body odour which has been my ointment and perfume suddenly changed to irritation!"

"Stop darling, when did you start feeling that from me? I am trying to work it out, whether these are due to my shortcomings, or perhaps some days when I don't bathe."

"Bathing or not, has got nothing to do with this. It is psychological and natural, and I cannot explain it." Without any argument or fight, I knew I had to find that out for myself. So I laughed and smiled to stop the argument.

"Now you know I am still the same, all we need is to sit down and talk and laugh and feel each other's comfort. One thing I know is that the devil cannot separate us," I continued.

"What about now, do you still get irritated with me?"

"Yes, but with toleration. I can endure it until you move away and do whatever you like, then I can smell fresh air."

"Is that why you were spitting?"

"Most probably yes. Sometimes if I perceive or smell you so much I vomit, which is not good for me."

"What can we do to stop it?" he asked.

"I don't know, it will stop when the time comes."

"How did you know?"

"I will ask the elderly," I said.

"These are the answers to all your questions; are you satisfied?" he replied.

"Yes, more than satisfied, and I am glad you are obsessed with love, and I promise to continue on the same level as you are. I LOVE YOU," I told him.

***

Chapter Thirty-Seven

Chief Hunter

She got up from my leg and walked away briskly. I was amazed at such a response coming from her, I thought to myself cautiously. I needed to sacrifice. I would pray, fast, kill a chicken for children to eat or give up smoking tobacco. I also realised that she had sacrificed herself to me, likewise I should make a sacrifice. Briskly, I called her in. She came to me with joy. "I would like to make a sacrifice to God for children to eat. I would like to kill a chicken cock and eat with some rice and a loaf of bread (akara)," I said. She was delighted and ready to cook it.

"When would you like to do it?" Tes asked.

"Tomorrow, before I go to the farm."

"All right." She was happy. Then she said, "your sadness has become happiness. Do you get it?"

I winked, she smiled and walked away. I now realised that women come to your life with a power to dwell in your home, and need more understanding to live with them.

People are getting excited. Children are shouting and full of happiness and some of them are crying not to go home, they wanted more time to spend and have more fun with each other. With me in the middle, they felt like spending the whole day here. One of the little girls came closer to me and said, "What is your name?"

"My name is Chief," all the children then said "Chief" and divided into groups of two to three and laughed.

So, I heard some of the group say, "His name is Chief," some who had lost their tooth said "thief", and they were correcting each other saying, "Chief, no say Chief and not thief!" until I eventually shrugged away. The same little girl asked again, "Is that your wife?" I said yes, she said, "She is pretty, people in the area said you married a pretty girl," and I responded "Thank you." "You are going to have a strong baby boy," she said, "because your wife is pregnant."

"How did you know?"

"She does not look the way she used to look."

I knew she was psychic and I must believe her, respect her, know her family and do something to help towards her growing up. Later in life her help would be glorious. I, however, was very happy to know, yet I still insisted to know her parents, because it seemed as though she was copy of my wife. "OK. Thank you. What is your name?"

"My name is Rola."

"What a beautiful name!"

"Thank you," she said and joined other children in her team. Looking towards my left side, I could see Tes looking at what we were doing, in fact she focused directly on me. "Are you OK, darling?" I asked

"Certainly, no problem, thank you." And she switched to the children's direction as if she was not purposely looking at me. "When are you going to finish with them? Because I need some time with my husband!" she exclaimed.

"Oh, oh, oh, darling, I should not be long. You can see they are getting tired now." Later in the afternoon when they all left and the whole surroundings and the house were quiet again.

"Tes," I called, "we have to continually be making sacrifice to God. When last have you made a sacrifice? Some people don't believe in it, but it is important. What about you, Si?"

"I don't know. Tes might know when last it was done. There was once, when I was there to eat and drink. But since I left to go to the King, I don't know anymore."

Tes moved closer and sat on my leg, "I have missed you," she uttered.

"I know, I can see it in your eyes." We kissed and romanced each other, feeling each other's comfort. When she saw Si coming back, Tes got up and asked if every plate and dishes have been washed and cleaned.

"Yes Ma."

"Thanks," she replied.

"It has been so long since I have seen you, Chief," said Si.

"Exactly Si, how are you and the palace?"

"We are all right and there is no problem. Thanks."

"How is my Little?"

"He is absolutely fine, recently he was talking about you that it has been long and the Hunters festival is approaching, that he may contact or see you in the farmhouse to know what would be going on. He sent you some killings; did Tes tell you?"

"Thank you very much, indeed yes she did. Can you please say thanks to him and say I really appreciated it?"

Si said, "OK."

"When you are ready to go home, give me a shout and I'll see you off at the junction," Tes replied.

"OK, Tes."

After a short while, I saw that Tes was miserable. I was concerned. So I pampered her as usual and put her to bed. I got ready for the farm. She slightly woke up as if she heard me talking to myself and she asked me, "Chief, when are you coming back?"

"Until I am able to fulfil my promise"

"See you darling" she said,

"Bye for now, my pretty," and I went out.

I could not connect my thoughts together on what Rola had said to me, until I reached the farmhouse, took a break and felt like dosing off. The thought came to me, I spelt it out, 'YOU – ARE – GOING – TO – HAVE – A – BABY – BOY.' No, she said, "You are going to have a '*strong* baby boy'." How did she know my wife is pregnant! Probably, she heard through the conversation from her parents, did she say that or I assumed? She could have said that my mum said your wife is pregnant and she is going to have a boy, but she didn't say that. She must be a psychic! No. I certainly needed to see the Chief Priest before the baby is born. Should that be the case, going hunting at the east side would be ideal.

I could not wait too long before I thought of going hunting. I took all the necessary things that I was supposed to have with me to get enough kills and went into the big bush so that I could find big animals to kill. Walking in the desert was so amazing because you needed to jog and run and hide and ambush, because some animals don't die easily, even if you are certain you have killed them, they still fight and destroy their surroundings before they give up.

However, I was hunting towards the east side of the town. I might as well take a detour around the bush as well before seeing the holy one. Moreover, if my wife had delivered the baby, I would hear about it, than to expect news being brought to my own farmhouse.

Since I've been making the sacrifices to god, whenever I fell asleep, I sometimes had a dream of being in the company of children, sometimes playing with them, beating them to cry or questioning them to say the truth. I sometimes cautioned them not to do it again and would wake up. All made me eager to pay the holy one a visit. He may get a lot of answers to all the above, rather than me wandering in the bush hunting without any kills and having anxiety.

***

Chapter Thirty-Eight

Chief Hunter

Far from squandering my mind, these thoughts brought relief. They enabled me to focus on my surrounding. A big rabbit. A big rodent. This will make a good kill. I paused to ambush the rabbit and the rodent which I happened to see at the same time. I took my small bow and arrow, aimed at the rabbit and got it without any hesitation. I aimed at the rodent that was having his dinner and he happily ended up in my sack, which had been empty for over half of the year now. I would not starve tonight because a rodent and a rabbit are enough for a lion, let alone only me.

The night went so well. With a good sleep and reserves in the bag, I headed to the holy one's house. He lived in the outskirts of the town. Whilst most people loved him, they didn't like to visit him. He lived in a thick forest where you cannot shout for help and get rescued, of course. It was about a mile to the town, built with a narrow road, like an elephant pathway. I was about to knock on his door, but it was already opened. He was astonished. "Chief, the big hunter, how are you and how is your wife, lovely Tes."

"She is very well, thank you."

"I hope nothing is wrong."

"Surely, nothing is wrong, just a couple of things or words which I found disturbing that brought me here."

"Without any waste of time, let us share then," the Chief priest replied. To give him more understanding, I started from how I knew Tes was pregnant; my irritation that she pushed me out of bed; my misgivings at being unable to get an animal to kill when other people get kills; the sacrifices made to God, and the reason for doing it; the little girl Rola's intuitions about the strong baby boy; likewise, my dreaming of playing with children.

In general, the holy man said at an early stage of pregnancy women get a lot of symptoms, some of them are regarding their men or husband. It's basic instinct and you cannot avoid it, all you need is understanding and to be supportive, be more helpful to the end, because this is the time she needs you most. If you are not there, she would have the baby and hold it herself, but when you are there, help counts. Therefore, that feeling is natural, it's love that makes the woman feel irrational about their husband. Some people may have morning sickness, they are unable to eat, vomiting delicious food after eating, eating something you and I would not like to eat. It is not forever; it is just a matter of time. Children are different to each other; therefore, their bodies are quite different to each other. How you feel during the first pregnancy is different to the second or third child being born.

"What can you do?" I asked.

The holy man said, "Nothing, absolutely nothing. Comfort her, don't force her to eat or drink, it's your love that wears down her body. The little girl profoundly knew that your wife is pregnant because being little and unknowing of

175

evil, she could see beyond the reasonable, like what you and I can see.

"Nothing to be afraid of, all these are such natural states of mind, when you are opened with your wife with one-mindedness, all this would be present. When the time comes, you will be successful in your hunting."

To clarify all what he said and if there was a known problem, he brought out 12 pieces of his dried kennel seeds. These were joined together by eleven pieces of strings. The space between each seed was about three inches long. He held the middle bit of four inches. He swerved it gently three times before he put it down on the floor. He usually read from this oracle, he understood it. He may ask you to go and make a sacrifice according to what it said. *Of course, that is where he got his inclination from* I thought. This is called opele.

He lifted his head up and said, "Big, you haven't got any known problem at all, you married a kind-hearted lady that will support you to the end. It says in the oracle. Here yourself take a careful look into it." I realised that surely, I should know about it because it was partially my dad's work. Sometimes, it is not everything you need to know about.

"Go with peace and peace will follow you, good man," the holy man said. I dipped into my sack and put the kill I brought for him on the floor. "You are always the same big hunter," he said, and I showed him the goodbye greeting. He smiled and I walked away into the bush behind his house.

All the way to the farmhouse, I could not get anything. This was unlike me. I even went into the top of the tree where you could hide and look at everything moving down below. The most I could kill were reptiles, even the common squirrel or squirrel monkeys I could not find. The situation was actually getting severe and intolerable for me.

I headed straight to my farmhouse and got some of my medicine that would enable me to see further. This I shouldn't have done, I became so distressed and all I could desire for was sleep, but I could not. I relaxed to settle down, yet my eagerness made me pathetic. I started to walk up and down in the farmhouse. *Why I am so pathetic and hallucinating?* I asked myself. I tried to settle down a bit, but the feeling became unbearable. Suddenly, I dozed away and saw Tes delivering, and within half a second my eyes wildly opened again. I knew something true had happened in my life, yet I did not know what.

The news came through this grapevine. *It was a boy,* I said to myself.

***

Chapter Thirty-Nine

Chief Hunter

"Praise, Praise, Praise!" I said and deep into my pocket, I brought out a big bunch of kola nuts and looked down under the kitchen area and found the pot of wine. I got myself a glass of wine and thanked my God for the great offering.

My problems were still unresolved, and I hadn't got any animal to kill. This time when going out, I had to use something different. I thought about it seriously, and after that I would be heading home to get a cuddle from my wife. This is whether I get a kill or not.

What a great shame! I headed home with nothing at all, not even a common rat, nothing. My sack became smelly, even everything I used to use now became smelly to me.

I entered home quietly; you would hardly know I had entered. Having put down my sack, I heard a baby crying, "Wai wai, wai, wai!" but the mother could not wake up. I carried the baby, looked into his eyes but I could not see anything, but visions of my father and ancestors, all I could assume was that the family has increased. "May God give you wisdom and make you like me and your mother. Amen." He stopped crying. Still holding him and I sat down beside Tes.

"How did you do?" Tes said briefly and was off asleep again. The baby was now smiling at me. I loved it, I smiled at him admiringly and he started to laugh. We both laughed until the mum became awake. He burst laughing again and I laughed back. "What is the matter with both of you laughing? What you both laughing at?" Tes asked.

"So, can you literally hear him laughing?"

"Of course, yes."

"Wonderful! I love him and that is my son. We have got a lot of things in common, beautiful." I put the baby down, put all my tools away and came back to bed. "When was the baby born?" I asked.

"Almost two weeks ago," she said as she was struggling to get the day and time and place. I furnished her with the exact day and time; she was flabbergasted and got out of bed to prepare for the morning breakfast and food for the baby boy too. Tes said, "I should not be surprised about you anymore; you are always like that, aren't you?" Briefly she looked at her surroundings and she asked, "Any killing this time?"

"No," I said. The baby was resting on my chest happily, while I used his mum's wrapper to cover us both.

According to tradition, it is shameful for someone, an important person of my calibre, to promise and not fulfil it. An outsider of your regime could come and make demands for your fulfilment. And it would be a disgrace to you and your family, somehow a series of it could lead to you relieved of your position in the community.

At this juncture, it was like a cockerel's crow sounding in my head, *the Hunter Festival is next month and would I be able to fulfil my vows to the people, or am I going to bring disgrace to this family regarding the tiger meat and stew that people are going to eat? Several times I have been to the tiger's environment, but I could not find any or see their footprints to trace them.* I was not as enthusiastic as I used to be. So, when Tes asked whether there is any killing this time? I shouted, "NO!"

"So, it would not be long before I get out of here," I continued.

"Why?"

"It doesn't seem my presence is required anymore."

"Don't be stupid, Chief, if I don't see you, then what about your son?" She dropped all whatever she was doing and rushed to my rescue. "Why do you say this?" she urged.

I'd already put the baby down, covered him properly and was about to leave the house, when I sat with my legs on the floor and bottom on the bed. She always sat on any available space on my body anyway. She knelt with her chest on my leg, I could feel the smell of jasmine and almond perfume she used, which made my body aroused. My mouth searched for her mouth; I was damned. Too randy. She tenderly pressed me down and she was simply on top this time. We both rolled to the left and right until I surrendered that she should remain on top. We both enjoyed it and were satisfied with the joy of sex.

"Why did you wait so long to have sex with me?" I asked.

She expressed calmly, "You need to understand your woman's call to mate, if not your woman would look at you as if you were just an animal who had no understanding, an uncivilised pervert! Women feel it the way you men have feeling, but you must know and understand our body language, when I want it, and when I don't. Sometimes it may be a coincident and we both want it at the same time, like we just did. It isn't bread you eat every day or food. It is an affection that is aroused through natural feeling of each other and the effect may result in cuddling, kissing, and depending on the state of mind and affairs of each, an intercourse occurs."

***

Chapter Forty

Chief Hunter

"You men always focus on your politics or business; you care less about the woman in the house or her state of affairs. Instead, you would bring your business or politics home to the woman. There is time for work, time to cry, and time to rejoice, likewise let work remain work and free up the few time left before you all go to bed. You should not neglect the family affairs, like the response you should make when your wife gets a new hairdo, or buys a new dress and desperately wants to wear it for you to see how beautiful she is. Where is your sense of humour? Of course, she always sleeps there like a log of wood, because she does not have an interest; did you romantically ask for it? How did you pursue the effect of having it?

"Remember, gone are the days that you were both boy and girl friends. Why are there sudden changes in the treatment of each other after marriage? It should not be changed. In fact, it should be joy and gladness for life," Tes said.

I was shocked because she had all the wisdom. I am very pleased to have married her. We ate our breakfast.

"I would be pleased if you could wake me up to go back," I said. She was pleased and let me sleep until the little boy woke me up by crying.

Before I went out she tried to remind me about the Hunter's Festival, the procedures and the importance of the occasion. I took in all that she said and her consideration for the occasion. I knew that if I'm not there, she would do everything as if I'm present. She knew about the procedure and with help from Deputy Chief Hunter and his wife, she would not be alone. So, I headed to the farm with courage and determination. Throughout that week I could not get a kill except some monkeys that I could use for dinner as well as sell pieces of their body parts in the market. These were quite peculiar to monkeys than any other animals, which were totally meant for consumption. Two weeks passed, and I knew I had to go to the palace to get the King's assent as to whether I will be able to give it to them or not, the tiger meat and stew. I don't know, but I have to use some of my power to get it for them.

Of course, I know I can be present in two places at the same time doing whatever is right for me, or to obtain what I want. I don't use this power often because it wears you out and makes you old quickly. While at the farm inspecting my crops, I was also at the King's palace discussing the Festival. As soon as I finished getting the King's approval at the palace, I disappeared smoothly into the air and appeared in the farmhouse.

I deliberately took a break from the bush and got some people in to help with harvesting and taking crops to the town. I took in three people, two men and a lady, so I could be able to have enough rest as well as doing more farming, growing more crops and harvesting cocoa, yam, coco yam, maize and beans. The Pawpaw Tree has all the ripest fruits and vegetables of different kinds. In fact, my stall would be the main focus of attraction because it will have it all, and I always get the best farmer of the year award. All these are part of the main festival, we are going to put our work on display from the morning of the festive night.

I had delegated the duties to them all and in most cases I didn't have to do too much because the people knew what they had to do. They were my labourers from times past, they knew me and I knew them. All tasks supposed to be done by Tes have been taken care of. I have got enough time to prepare myself for the big hunting as well equip myself to face any eventualities.

I overheard that the preparation was going on fantastically. Tes does not take it hard, regardless of my misfortune (unable to get killings), she prepared as if nothing was wrong. I could see that people were appreciating her and bringing her gifts and ointment for the baby, some she used and some were being kept till I return home. "Beautiful wife," I said, "never trust people with gifts, because they will give you some ridiculous gifts."

My preparation with potions was getting too much. *I must make it small because I am now a family man with child*, I said to myself. It's only for the bush. I must not forget to take them off immediately when I am about to enter the town. I realised that some children may love to come and hug me, especially women. Good, I said to myself, and I've got to hunt quickly. My job has increased considerably because of Tes. The more I want to do something quickly, the more I get set back when I realise she would have done this if she was with me at the farmhouse. Therefore, I have to do it all.

***

Chapter Forty-One

Chief Hunter

As the sun set, I set off into the thick rainforest with a bow and arrow, shotgun and my rod. As I entered, I found some big snails. I picked them up as I was walking, chopped off the bottom point to drink the greyish juice, the blood, that comes out from them. This tasted natural, splendid and enabled me to calm down. I drank two snails' juices. Having had enough, I continued onwards, searching and making ambushes when necessary because the big cats were very dangerous – they could stalk you for miles until they caught you. Yet I couldn't find any animals, although I knew if I could find antelopes, surely a tiger must be somewhere around, else I would just be wandering without anything.

I was almost close to exhaustion and it was getting too dark; you hardly heard any sound except the hissing sounds of insects along the riversides. It must be around the third hour of the morning, I reckoned. Suddenly, I heard someone say, "Who are you prodding in my sight without regard to my excellence? Who are you?" repeatedly. Whoever it is, they must be talking to me. "Can you come closer to me? You ou ouou," it continued. I was shocked and felt so little, I looked right and in front about 50 yards away, I saw nothing. The darkness of this site was too extreme but you noticed that the sound and the image was from there. This was the Bush Goddess. As I moved 10 yards closer and stopped, she started asking question after question. "What do you want? You have been stepping on my toes so many times. Can you answer me?"

"I am Di, the Chief Hunter, looking for a tiger to kill in the celebration of our annual festival."

"Why do you want a tiger?"

"It's a vow which I had committed myself into, made to the whole town, that if I have a baby, I would give them a taste of tiger's stew – a promise to the masses. Isn't that too ambitious a promise?"

"Yes," the Goddess said.

"Now comes the time to fulfil the promise, and I have been going up and down all these days looking for a tiger to kill and have found no animals, let alone a substitute.

"All right, I am going to do you a big favour, OK," the Goddess said. "You must not tell anybody about it, do you promise?"

"Yes, Goddess," I said.

"Look to your right side, see the first oak tree? Now look at the second oak that has a shrub next to it. Underneath the dead oak tree that has fallen down is a big stone cave door in which live a tiger and two tiger cubs. Their mum has been away for one or two days now, she hasn't come back. Go and take them for your use."

Within a second of hearing these words, the atmosphere became brightened again and you could see the area was cleared. I felt excitement but I tried not to rush to get the direction right. Moreover, I had to be careful; a tiger is such an elusive animal, she may be hiding with the cubs and prove to be difficult to find. I looked forward; I could see the two tiger cubs playing on top of the large stone; they were about two years old, almost adult tigers that would soon leave their parent. *Perhaps the mum has abandoned them*, I thought.

Apparently, I found, I was not the only one who is interested in the tiger cubs; the other was the biggest python I had ever seen in my life. It was slithering ahead to take one of the cubs who were just playing. Suddenly, one of the tiger cubs stopped, paused and struck the python, then I saw the python's head camouflaged with the surroundings. I took my long rod and used it on both of their heads. The second cub ran inside the hole but smoothly and efficiently, I used an arrow on him. It took him from behind and he was dead in the doorway that led into the cave.

I was very, very happy. I was standing and jumping in jubilation, then I took a second look at the python. The long serpent was huge and fat and would be goddamn too heavy for me to carry. I burst laughing again and again, saying many thanks to the Goddess. The tigers were heavy too but I would carry them home, I promised. An instinct told me you need to move the python away from there, else you may not find it when you come back. Tigers never leave their kids, so never ever could I think the cubs' mum would return to the stone.

Time was running away from me. I tried as much as possible to put the python around my body, but it didn't work. I took my cutlass, cut two thick wood pieces and made a push carriage, then moved all the animals into it and headed home, in the main town. As I was about to reach home, around two to three miles away, I found somewhere to keep the python and covered it with two banana leaves and put the marks of appear and disappear on it. For whoever coming to collect it, if he is a hunter, he would surely find it; if not a hunter, I would need to give some explanations before the person could find it.

As I was nearing home, I had been hearing the sounds of drumming, I disengaged myself from the strong medication which I was wearing and, of course, became visible. This I did with the use of snail blood. I smashed the pointed bum of a snail and let the blood drain into my mouth; the taste was sour not sweet but relaxed the body muscles. I indeed liked snail blood, at times I used it as my sweets. Quickly, my body felt lighter and relaxed, not heavy as it was before. If I waited a bit longer, I would sleep here; so I made no mistake of resting at all I just headed home.

***

Chapter Forty-Two

Chief Hunter

The remedy for what I had use was to rest and that was why I would sleep as if there was no tomorrow. The closer I walked to the town, the louder the sound and noise of the people were. This, however, made me happier and more so because I was able to fulfil the promise I had made. I was thanking the 'Bush Goddess'; likewise, I questioned whether I would meet the tigress on my way. Since I was a short distance to the town, there should be no problem. Surely, it seems I was right, as I came near the bottom end of the road close to Little Hunter's house down to the junction close to my house, I heard people shouting, "The Chief is here, here he comes!" Quickly, the news spread to Tes, and the baby boy, and all the hunters knew I was around.

"Let some people go and meet him," I was told my Deputy said but absolutely no one except Little Hunter volunteered, he himself felt awkward but he had to, without people knowing he did not like it. Simply because most of them knew how difficult it was to meet me, they could be playing with their lives.

Instantly, I saw him coming with two big men; one of them was a friend and the second was the junior brother to the

Deputy Chief Hunter. Instead of them hugging me, I hugged them first and the Little Hunter then knew I was not having something that could harm them. He was full of enthusiasm, he danced and danced and shoved his bum at me as a good gestured greeting. I was glad that he took the sack that contained the killed tigers from me. I said to the other two, "Why don't you fellows go to the bush about a mile, you will find one of the kills there, and let this man wait to carry this hefty bag home. I will send him back to you with another hand, because I think that kill would be too heavy for two people to carry."

"No, Chief," Little said, "just him would be enough in case more hands would be needed to carry the rest of the kill we have here." Without hesitation the drummers started using the drumming to call my name, and speaking in incantations. I could see some elderly women were dancing towards me to welcome me home. While women were dancing at the left, men were dancing at the right; they all came and the men carried me, lifted me high up in the air until we reached home – they did not let me walk. In fact, I was more than excited about the whole show and I was full of joy. When they reached where I would sit, they threw me up three times and caught me before they put me down on my seat. The man who carried the kill home was the one that called his friend to help get something from the bush for the Chief; he was more than delighted to help, and Little Hunter followed.

In the bush, the Little Hunter knew what he had to do to get the kill, if not they would be there till tomorrow evening and would not find anything. He saw my sign and removed it to trace where the kill was kept. He could not believe his eyes that a snake could be that big. All of them were watching with excitement. Could they move it? No. Until two other men came to join them, only then were they able to lift it up. Of course, the Little Hunter was not any good for them, because his height was too short to lift in front or in the middle or behind at its tail. The Little Hunter was not any good other than to kill insects that landed on the python's body.

As they entered the town, people including children were following them watching where they were going with the big snake. Some of the boys who were tall enough helped them to lift the tail to the destination, where the snake would be burned and the skin she was wearing removed. And of course, the python skins have been used for many purposes, namely medicinal and treasured wear for the King and Knights. Women often used it to symbolise their status in the community, like the Princess, especially the first child and first daughter of the King. However, I showed the people where to put the snake and called others who would help to remove the skin without making any hole in it and told them that after they should pass the meat to the women for cooking, that is Tes. The men were relieved and joined the ceremony. Little found his colleagues.

At home, I showed the people where they should burn and remove the tiger cubs' skins. One should get the skin removed and the second should get the skin burnt. As they were on the ground, people had gathered to look at the tiger and discuss the exclusive animal. Later, one of the children who had got the nerve went to touch the tiger on the ground and the tiger roared. Everyone there was scared. Even some of the elders around were afraid and asked me to shoot it as it was not dead. "No," I said, and I told him to put the gun away. Because a dead tiger is a tiger until you burn it or cut its body, then she would stop roaring.

It was my duty to address them and all knew that my promise had been fulfilled today. Looking around me, I realised that my wife wasn't around to meet me at the dance or at the big table. I rushed inside to see if something was wrong. There I found her, where she laid down with the baby, sobbing. "What is the matter?" I asked. I lifted her head up on my lap. "What is the matter? Tell me," I asked again.

She said, "I have been stranded in here since yesterday; this baby didn't sleep, and I have only been able to ask your Deputy's wife to do small tasks but most of what I was supposed to do have been taken over by Si where my presence was needed."

"Mm! Mm, is that all?" I lowered down and gave her a kiss and kissed the baby too. "Here I am now, why don't you come out with me; we should show the world our baby, everybody wants to see you. Let them know you are all right; we have a bouncing baby boy." She rose up, washed her face. The baby gradually opened his eyes and he smiled at me, I lifted him up and gave him a kiss. We went out with the rest of our friends and family that were inside, and they joined in the singing, happy to see Tes and the baby. Those who had longed to see her now had the pleasure and joy of seeing her with the baby.

"What is the child's name?" asked one of the audience.

"His name is Ode-Kunte."

"Pleasant name, especially for these occasions."

"Many thanks," I said, "Let the party begin."

All shouted in joy. We began the ceremony by making the sacrifice to the God of Iron. As soon as we beheaded the first dog, people shouted 'Ogun ye ye ye', which means the God of Iron exists, the second and the third dog were sacrificed at the four corners of the town. With my child in my hand, I danced with him and prayed as we moved from one place to another, until we went back to the big ground where the ceremony and performance would take place.

***

Chapter Forty-Three

"In The Bush!" (Part 1)

In the bush where the tiger cubs were killed, the tigress came back and looked for her children. She called, cried and was restless because of the two children had disappeared; the whole environment became unbearable because of the children. The kill she made became useless, as she had tried to make a kill so the cubs didn't go hungry. She tried to look for the python and other cat leopard but she could not find them around, so she was worried. Her unrest became disturbing to everyone in the bush and the area became unbearable, even the birds that flew in the sky knew something was wrong downstairs. Bush Goddess intervened with a loud voice, "Who is that causing unnecessary disturbances over there, what is the problem? What is your problem, can you be civilised, can you talk to me right now?"

"Who are you?" Question upon questions waiting, many quick answers to be heard. "It's me, My 'Lord'," the Tigress responded.

"Who is me?"

"Your most favourite King of the jungle," it began annotating herself as a city built on the hilltop which cannot be hidden, "the one and only one who is the king in front of you, lord."

"What is your problem?"

"Another two of my children have disappeared again; where do they go? My Lord, if they are dead, I will find their bodies. If they went playing, they should be back by now."

"Do you want to know where they are?"

"Yes, My Lord."

The Goddess shouted with a louder voice than her own voice, "The Chief Hunter came looking for you, he would have killed you for the naming ceremony of his first child; he had promised his people he would make a sacrifice of a tiger to God if his wife had a baby."

"Ridiculous and unbearable! Using me! Even taking my children to sacrifice to God. To you?"

"No ooo oo, not me."

"What did he think in his mind? Is he mental! Did he think I am a goat, pig, chicken, cow or what? Okay, thank you," the Tigress said to the Bush Goddess, and she continued, "The Chief Hunter shall see what I would do to him and you will hear about it. All these days and years I have been watching him; I didn't want any confrontation with human. But now that the human needs my confrontation, so be it." She said bye to the Bush Goddess and they both disappeared.

The tigress was furious, fuming and about to burst with anger.

She made her way to the town, saying to herself, that there is no mercy for someone who dares use your child for a sacrifice. I do not care whoever it is, I would rip his skull off his neck and his brain would I bring out and use for my dessert, so shall be the end of the stupid Chief Hunter. He does not have mercy for my children and likewise, I would not have mercy for his child; both of them are dead.

As she was going, she stopped at the First Banana tree and asked to borrow cloth as she had a special occasion to attend at the town and would need to look her best. First Banana showed how she looked presently and how she would look when he finished her make-up. "Good," the Tigress said when she looked in the mirror.

Then First Banana finished her make-up. She was gorgeous, the sight of her was tantalising. The breasts were pointing like the tips of arrows, her shoes gave more to the height, which made her normal height adequate, her hips were parallel to the bottom; therefore, she did not have too big a bum. The skirt was kinky, an immaculate dress that would make men commit themselves; her blouse was black, a mixture with gold and silver shining through. The round neck of the blouse revealed the 22-carat gold pendant jewellery. Her handbag was not too small or big but perfectly matched with her dressing.

So, she came out of the bush as if someone who had just went to relieve herself in the modern English toilet. The passers-by looked at her and her exotic hairstyle in ecstasy. "I think she is exotic," men said to each other, none could confront her or say hello to her, they were just looking with their mouths wide open. She had gone before they could talk to each other. "Where is she going?" they asked each other.

Some of them were stalking her while some of them were in general walking to the festival venue. Those who are stalking intended to know who she was going to meet among the audiences or spectators, because she was too beautiful and

197

there was no one to be compared with her except Tes, the Chief Hunter's wife.

Apparently, everyone had to pass through where the tiger skins were on display to dry in the sun. They were guided by two hefty men who were to show exaggeratedly how the Chief Hunter killed the exclusive animal, the tiger. As soon as she approached, she could see the skins of her cubs being displayed in the sun. She stopped and said, "Very beautiful!"

One of the men responded, "Yes, very, very beautiful like yourself."

She smiled and asked, "How many of them do you have?"

"Our Chief killed two of them; the other one is being burnt in the fire."

***

Chapter Forty-Four

"The Tigress at Chief Hunter's Home"

Her anger almost came through but the human skin she was wearing kept suppressing her nerves' reaction. Every time she tried to react as a tiger the human skin suppressed it. She was in the deepest thought; she would need to bring the Chief Hunter out to the bush for killing.

As she approached the venue, it was the Little Hunter that spotted her, and he did not hesitate to ask where she wanted to go. "Good day," the tigress lady said to the Little Hunter.

He was full of honour and amazement and said, "Good day to you."

"Can you take me to the Chief Hunter, please?"

The Little Hunter was mesmerised by her tone of voice and could not say no to a beautiful lady, but a slight suspicion arose – was there something unusual about her? He asked, "Any particular problem?"

She said, "No!" instantly.

"Are you a friend?"

She smiled a smile that made the Little Hunter forget the ingenuity in her. "Yes, I am the wife's friend," she said.

Little Hunter smiled back and took her to where the Chief Hunter was sitting helping the family feed the baby.

Tes was the first to say hello. The Chief Hunter had to get up to allow her to sit down with the baby. Chief Hunter refused to give the baby for her to carry but allowed her to just peck the baby with her right hand on the baby's left cheek. The Chief, briefly saw her fingernail grow long, sharpened and then it suddenly disappeared. This aroused suspicion in him.

They looked at each other's faces, but the tigress lady looked up at the Chief with a smiling face. Then the Chief Hunter, seemed to calm down and smiled back with good gesture, saying. "Sit down here, it is our festival day; therefore, you meet us so very well."

"The baby looks like you," she said.

"Thank you," replied the Chief.

She was entertained with a lot of food and meat to eat, but she was not comfortable sitting with the family at all. Every second she felt unrest and wanted to fight, especially looking at Tes, because Tes did not let her out of her sight. She must have understood. So it wasn't long before that the Tigress asked the Chief Hunter to excuse her as she would like to go home now. The Chief Hunter requested that they should get a leaf and put some food wrapped up with the leaf in a small bag for her to take home and eat. She showed her appreciation for the food, took it and stepped out of the house while noticing that the Chief Hunter showed no intention to see her off the road.

Tes purposely requested the Chief, "Wouldn't you see her off? After all she is a lady, be civilised." Tes called the Chief back, who was about to leave without any protection at all.

Then Chief took his armband and wore it and was about to get through the door when the wife called him back and wondered if that wasn't enough protection? He came back a second time and took his little rod and wore his blood-soaked and dried wrapper around his waist and got going. The third time she called him back again, "Chief, that is not enough you cannot see someone you don't know or have not met before without taking your rod," Tes went further and said, "Look, the Pope wears his cross when going out, the Muslim takes his prayer bead. You are a hunter, what have you got? You have got your 'rod', why don't you get inside and take your rod with you?" Then Chief knew this time he had to take his long rod.

When Tes saw her husband dressing as if he was going to war, she believed her husband was as strong as a stone and nothing could all of a sudden happen to him. He would come back home alive, so she stopped lamenting. But the Tigress lady did not like the idea of his dressing up. She voiced out wickedly, "You are only seeing me off the road and you are dressing as if you are going to war."

Looking up at her you could see the seriousness in her, her voice was trembling, her face was frowning with displeasure and was crooked. Chief shrugged and followed her; in fact, he wanted Little Hunter to follow him. The tigress absolutely refused that. Chief did not like the idea; however, they got going because of the time, he didn't want it to get darker and she was a woman.

Each time he wanted to get back, she refused and said, "How could you let a woman off here. Suppose I am your wife, would you leave me alone here?" She persisted saying that when she was ready to let him go back, she would be the one to tell him. Chief didn't like it because there was no quickest way to the town where she was taking him. Yet, she became one who must be obeyed.

His heart froze, not knowing what to do, he dipped into his wrapper and got out a guinea pepper with an old kola nut and his heart woke up again. He vividly knew there was going to be trouble, what trouble he didn't know. So, he tapped his wrapper, disappeared and became a fly. He came back quickly because he thought there was no reason for this. As soon as they reached the First Banana tree, she said in a commanding tone of voice, "Wait there I am coming, I would like to pee."

Within a few minutes, it was the surprise of his life – right in front of him was a big tiger coming towards him. He tapped his wrapper and became a fly again; he flew to the exact point where he met the 'Bush Goddess' last time. Suddenly he was back as himself and here was the tiger lamenting, "Bring back my two cubs, else you are dead! You son of a bitch!" she roared at the top of her voice. Then she repeated, "Where are my children? Bring them back now." She scratched his arm and his leg with her hand and she roared again and again.

***

Chapter Forty-Five

"In the Bush!" (Part 2)

The Bush Goddess answered, "Who are youuuuu, shouting in my world?

"Why are you so loud in my forest without regard for my existence?"

"It is me the tiger and say no more," the Tigress ordered. "I brought him back here to be killed right in front of you. When he killed my children, you knew and you did not do anything to help. I knew my children would be shouting for help and you would not do anything. He wanted to disappear, and he does not know I am more intelligent than him. I brought him back here and I wanted to finish him right here, right now."

"Please don't, before you do that both of you need to speak to me and to the ground, because you all will be buried in the ground, so can you please present your report to the ground in detail?" The Chief wanted to go first.

She said, "No!" and gave the Chief Hunter three scratches on his left cheek, blood started coming out. "You have not seen anything yet," she said. As she was reporting to the ground, the 'Bush Goddess' winked at him and said, "Use your rod." In his aggression he used the long rod on her head three times. Her head busted and the brain splattered outside. She was crying "mh-mmm, mh-mmm", three times she stretched, her two legs moved towards the front and then backwards and she went dead.

This time the Bush Goddess did not disappear. She waited a bit for him to say goodbye, and told him to keep up the good work, and that his sacrifice to God is essential and disappeared.

He was still in a shock, looking in front of him, he went and sat down on the big stone for a couple of minutes to relax and consume some fresh air. He thought how to carry it home. It would be ideal to build a push carriage, the type he built for the cubs. He pulled it for two miles and then was tired. "Hold on," he said to himself, covering it exactly the same way he covered the snake and thought to get some people to fetch it.

At the junction, as soon as he reached the road, everyone was excited because they were all waiting to see him. Also because they wondered what could have happened with a man seeing off a woman down the road. He asked for his Deputy to take someone and get the kill home. While the Little Hunter stayed behind to serve him.

This time the news about his second killing spread to the whole town, that he had just seen off a woman and on his way back killed a very large tiger. News spread to the King's palace that he has killed another tiger. What the King had never done before was to spare the time and come back again to the festival. Soon he got the information that the King was on his way again and would like to see the large tiger. More preparations were undertaken. He asked Tes, Si and Vi, a lady from the palace, and the rest to dance and bring King to the venue.

This time he knew his wife and child would have no trouble or problems at all; Tes only quivered when she heard that lady had proclaimed to be her friend.

***

Chapter Forty-Six

"At Home – When Chief Hunter First Brought the Tiger Cubs" Chief Hunter's Wife, Tes

The King danced and witnessed some of the performances both from home and other towns that were closed to us. Not so long after, he left to go home. I was surprised since it seemed to be very early for him to leave, but since I'd heard about his state of health, I could not be bothered to stop him. Frankly, he should know better.

Si was on her way looking for me. She asked the Deputy Chief Hunter's wife, "Where is Tes?" Then she looked down, there was I dancing.

"Why are you looking for Tes?" Deputy Hunter's wife asked.

"You can see the baby cry the hell out. The more I attempted to make him feel all right the more he cried. He may need the parent to breastfeed him now. I don't know, I cannot continue carrying him everywhere when he is crying like this."

I looked at his face. He stopped and suddenly started to cry again. I took the baby from Si and said, "Go away both of you and do what you are supposed to be doing." I went inside with the baby. I now figured out what exactly was making him cry. Whenever the baby heard the voice of his dad, he would start crying, because he was looking for his dad to carry him. Even if he heard the step of his father coming he would cry, and if he did not come and pick him, he would cry more and more.

"Something bad must have happened," I said. The way I suddenly felt was not a good sign from my body at all, so I took my son and went into the bedroom and lay down with the baby sucking my breast. Still he cried. I cried till I got a feverish cold, and then I dosed away and two things came in to my sleep. I woke up when Chief Hunter came inside to the bedroom. Through my dream I got to know that my son is not an ordinary boy but a powerful boy who would soon show what he is capable of doing. The second was a visitor, an incredible one, whether for me or for Chief Hunter, I don't know, but one of us is going to receive a visitor."

This time Chief intended to take our son, Odekunte, out, but I said to him, "No, why don't you go away and allow him to sleep?"

"I think he needs it," said Chief Hunter and so we went out with the baby to watch the fascinating performances and activities from our neighbouring cities.

Yet I could not concentrate with the activities but had to dash inside to see my family, then the Little Hunter brought a beautiful lady into our parlour. We served her food and meat.

"Yes," I said.

"Do you know that I have got a strong and powerful boy?" Chief boasted.

"Yes, of course, who did you think he will resemble?" I replied.

"I think if he resembles the mother, he will be strong and a little bit short, and if he resembles the father he would be strong and powerful."

"Where did you get your intuition from?"

"Through my special way of thinking and that is an old saying."

The Festival went well, most were on their way home and Chief Hunter saw that beautiful lady to the end of the road. I told him to wear all his gear. He should be home by now.

***

Chapter Forty-Seven

"Promises – On the Way To The Bush With The Tigress" Chief Hunter

I promised that 'if my wife becomes pregnant and has the child' in the same year as the festival, I would celebrate the birth of the baby with the killing of a tiger for people to eat tiger meat and stew. Isn't it ambiguous – forgetting that having a child and killing a tiger are two different things?

If you have a wife, one day a baby will arrive. But it takes wisdom to kill a tiger because nobody wants to die, including the animal. Moreover, why promise a tiger when you can easily kill a rabbit, chicken or an antelope, which often taste equally as delicious.

Killing a tiger is as hard as killing honeybees, due to its stealth, camouflage, stalking, his angry face, and ambushing skills. He is one of the top predators. However, killing a tiger as I did, makes me feel big among my fellow hunters. I am superior. The top hunter. My name and voice will be heard in the palace, in the town and within my community. Else there was no point looking for a tiger to kill when you can seriously kill a chicken!

Tes called me back three times for my rod and gear, regardless of the fact that I don't think I would ever be in extreme trouble.

For merely seeing someone just off the road, I had to wear all these. I don't like it, but she has demanded it. The more I want to go back home, the more this lady persist in asking why I won't help her further down the river. "You would not be long going back to meet your lovely baby," so she kept saying.

So I accompanied her further until we came to the river where she excused herself to wee. A very big tiger has jumped out from the bush, nearly crushing me down, and right in front of me, demanding that I should bring her children back, "else today you will die in the same way as you killed my children. Where are my children?" it asked again in an agonised voice. It is dragging me into the bush, towards the place where I killed the cubs. I have never felt so little before or been pushed like this in my entire life.

I was shivering and could not think of what I should do. My brain went dead. It's screaming. I thought I should better wake up and do something, then I heard the voice of the Goddess saying, "Use your rod on her head." Without any hesitation, I could not waste time, my long rod met her head. She wanted to bite my hand off. I used it again and she was quiet, I knew she was dead.

Then after this, I suddenly fell asleep and within a minute I awoke and thought to myself I needed to listen to my wife, she just saved me from the evil predator, else I could also have been her special dinner. She might not even eat me but leave the dead body to rot. For I listened to my wife Tes, my life was saved.

Nearly the End

The story my father told me was still so vivid in mind. Then my dad said, "So you see my son, there are many things which you must learn as man intending to take a wife and many lessons one can learn here." He recounted the story, "Tes, a hunter's wife. She's remarkably wise. Especially when the husband, the Chief Hunter, was about to see the special visitor off..." as he trailed on my mind drifted to whether I would have lunch today or not. I couldn't play with my brothers, but I thought to myself, it wouldn't be good if I did not share this story.

My dad's eyes focused on mine, and he looked at me seriously. So I refused to let my mind wonder off, it was as though he was scanning my brain to see if there were any distractions. I cleared my brain; I couldn't take the chance of receiving a dirty slap. I focused the pen on the paper, and then he said, "Women – they are our mothers, and men should cherish them. When you are with them, you feel on top of the world. If you don't have a wife, you know something is missing in your life. Have a wife or live your life as a bachelor. I believe the blessings of marriages are in three folds. First, you are no more alone. We multiply and extend and we are addressed as Mr and Mrs. Secondly, there is security, safety and protection. Thirdly, there is a helper in the house and jobs are done more efficiently because there are two. You know, a job done together can bring blossoms. These are the combination of blessings you get from a marriage."

I did not know what he meant, at least we're finished. "Thank you, Pa," I said. It's time to go and play; I want to be as strong as Chief Hunter.

The End.